The Man in the Lake

Gun shook his head to throw the water from his eyes, pulled in a heavy lungful of air and dove again.

Ten feet below he reached the Buick and opened the door. Larson was stiff in his sitting position, looking straight up through the custom sunroof. His hands floated an inch above his lap and Gun saw that several fingers were missing, cleanly nipped at the second joints.

Air. With the blood going sluggish in his arteries, Gun pulled. The commissioner's legs cleared the steering wheel and Gun gripped a solid thigh and shoved the body skyward. Larson drifted up through twilight, legs straight out front, face turned up. He spun slowly as he rose . . .

COMEBACK

L.L. ENGER

POCKET BOOKS

New York   London   Toronto   Sydney   Tokyo   Singapore

An *Original* Publication of POCKET BOOKS

POCKET BOOKS, a division of Simon & Schuster Inc.
1230 Avenue of the Americas, New York, NY 10020

ISBN: 0-671-70918-6

First Pocket Books printing August 1990

10 9 8 7 6 5 4 3 2 1

POCKET and colophon are registered trademarks of
Simon & Schuster Inc.

Printed in the U.S.A.

To Kathy and Robin.
For the long silent evenings.

COMEBACK

Prologue

1980

On the evening of August 17 something over twenty million people learned of Gun Pedersen's sudden retirement from baseball. John Chancellor told them about it on the NBC *Nightly News,* a program not known for its attention to sports figures. Mr. Chancellor did a fair and workmanlike job with the story. He used a tone of sadness, respect for the fallen. He applied a cool network gloss over the sordid parts.

"Major league baseball lost a hero today," he began, "when Gun Pedersen, the Detroit Tigers' prized and beleaguered left fielder, walked away from the game." Behind Mr. Chancellor's left shoulder a picture of Gun Pedersen appeared, the Topps baseball card from his rookie year. The dark-billed cap with the baroque capital D shaded a young face with high cheekbones and a serious set to the eyes.

"Just three days after attending the funeral of his wife, who was killed in the tragic crash of Flight 347 in Wisconsin, Pedersen told NBC this afternoon he's played his last game.

1

"The season isn't over, of course, but Pedersen seemed headed for the kind of year most veterans his age can only wish for. He led his teammates in home runs and batting average, and was voted the American League's starting All-Star left fielder for the twelfth time in seventeen seasons. For the past two weeks, though, the normally quiet-mannered Pedersen has been the focus of headlines for his actions *off* the field. Press reports of his relationship with film star Susannah Duprey"—on screen now, the soundless clip of a sleek, dark-haired woman mouthing words at a thicket of microphones—"were followed by the on-camera fistwork Pedersen performed on the reporter for *American Mirror,* a New York–based tabloid program." Another clip flashed on the screen, and a man vast of width took two short blows, to the gut and chin, then rolled sideways onto the hood of a parked car.

The clip ended and John Chancellor was back. "These events shocked a nation of baseball fans. Then came the plane crash. Now it is over. Inside of one week, Gun Pedersen has buried his wife, his career, and a little of the innocence and honor that have always belonged to the national pastime." Chancellor paused, seemed to frown at a paper on his desk. He looked up at the camera. "We asked Mr. Pedersen by telephone what he intends to do now. His answer, and I quote: 'I'm going north.'" A pause. "That's the NBC *Nightly News.* This is John Chancellor. Good night."

1990

Sometimes it seemed like he hadn't gone far enough north.

The first year, living in the log house he'd built for Amanda as a summer place in the early sixties, he'd been tempted to rip the phone out and toss it off the dock into Stony Lake. This was northern Minnesota and his number was unlisted, but people still got it: guys calling up and saying, Get back to the game, man—sorry about your wife, but let's not quit baseball, not the important stuff. Others called to say, You've sinned, buddy, and you're going to Hell in a sled you've built yourself. One woman phoned from a group called Females for Fidelity, saying she understood the pressures on professional athletes and was willing to come give him personal support and consolation. He changed his number four times that first year.

It got better after that. Gun put a new roof on the house, replaced some logs that boarded termites, and made enough quiet trips into the little town of Stony so that people nodded to him now and didn't just stare. Meanwhile the sportswriters found other sensations and misfortunes to use up, and the phone rang less and less often.

Gun drank coffee in the town bakery sometimes, and the men from the grocery and the hardware store and the bank who always seemed to be there were glad to see him. He started getting phone calls from local politicians. A state representative wanted his endorsement on a school sports bill; the mayor wanted to post a Home of Gun Pedersen sign at the Stony city limit. He said no, of course; caution was habitual. Then the Loon Country Attractions thing came up.

Loon Country was the idea of Stony's only certifiable rich man, Lyle Hedman of the Hedman Paper Mill. It would be Minnesota's answer to Disneyland, he said; a high-rise, high-tech island of prosperity in the middle of unemployed northern Minnesota. An amusement park. A convention center. The biggest shopping mall for two hundred miles, any direction. It would sit right next to the big blue water, Stony Lake, and fill the town with business and happiness. Lyle Hedman said so to Gun, and wondered if Gun would like a job putting his face on freeway billboards. Gun said he wouldn't, and then he learned that when it counted, people could still remember the bad stuff.

"You know, Gun, this could be a positive thing for you," Hedman said.

"Positive?"

"Well, yes." Lyle coughed over the phone, and Gun understood. "You had a bit of a rough outing your last time in the public eye."

"No thanks, Lyle." Gun hung up.

Then the conservation group called. Save the Lake. They were the ones who worried Loon Country Attractions would send too much sewage and poison into the water. Gun agreed with them. But they remembered too.

"We think your help on this important issue could be beneficial all around. It'll give us a spokesman people will recognize, and give you some very good publicity," the county commissioner said.

"I'm not looking for publicity," Gun told him.

"No, no, but surely it wouldn't hurt, not after . . ."

"Yes?"

"Not after what happened before. Seems to me you'd want to put your name on something folks can respect."

Gun hung up again. He pulled tobacco and papers from the pocket of his flannel shirt and rolled a smoke at the kitchen table. He toyed with the wooden matches, arranging them there in the shape of a baseball diamond.

Redemption, he realized, might still be a chilly ways distant.

Gun Pedersen stood in the shadow of a white pine, sixty feet six inches from his home-built pitching machine. He waited in longjohns and red tennis shoes, the long blond Hillerich and Bradsby resting lightly on his bare shoulder. The metal arm of the machine inched upward, ticking. Gun lifted the bat, tensed the muscles of his back and arms, narrowed his eyes. He relaxed his fingers on the smooth handle. The arm reached horizontal in its rising motion. Gun wiggled the tip of the bat. The arm snapped forward and the ball came straight and fast, waist high. He took a quick short stride and swung hard. His eyes held the ball until contact and he felt the clean wooden pop. The line drive took off low and whined with the full thrust of Gun's swing. The ball was still rising when it hit the trunk of a pine tree in what would have been deep left field in a ball park.

"Robbed," Gun said.

Tapping the flat white stone he used for home plate

with the fat end of his narrow-handled bat, he rolled his shoulders in a shrug. He never granted himself his morning swim until he'd hit three baseballs into Stony Lake, which lay 380 feet due east, never felt completely ready for a day until he'd taken his swings. Some guys, of course, had to have their juice, and Gun granted them that. Others just threw money at shrinks, poor bastards. But Gun had his tonic too, and knew it. Every morning as he loaded the pitching machine, in his mind he loaded each ball with something he wanted to forget: Hedman's mall project, his daughter Mazy's anger (which she had every reason to hang on to), the mistakes from his old life that people liked to remind him of. Then he watched these freighted balls come floating toward him, and jacked each one to kingdom come and gone.

He did a deep knee bend, straightened up slowly— all six feet, six inches of him—and rested the bat once more on his shoulder. Again the metal arm ticked upward. In his peripheral vision he saw his World Series ring glinting in the new sun. He wiggled his bat. From behind him came the sound of a vehicle coming up the pitted gravel driveway: a creaky, loose-jointed truck, cylinders missing badly. Gun sighed. That would be Bowser. The metal arm snapped and Gun strode into the ball, releasing his level, whipping swing. Again the pop of wood on leather, again the rising line drive. Only this time the ball found its way through the sky full of pines, reached its highest point of flight well over the lake, and finally dropped, putting a circular scar in the water's perfect mirror of the sky.

"There." He leaned the bat against the nearest tree and turned to look at the fat man spilling out the driver's side of a Chevy spotted with rust holes the size of dinner plates. Gun shook his head and started toward him, moving with the easy grace of a large man

8

whose heart and lungs are more than big enough to handle his size.

"Gun Pedersen, Gawd damnit, you owe me!" Bowser Devitz was the son of old Jeremy Devitz, and Gun understood his complaint. It was the Devitz property, a hundred sixty acres of low trees and marsh, that Hedman had bought for his mall project.

"Gun Pedersen—"

"Yeah, Bowser." Gun raised a calming hand.

Bowser marched right up to Gun and stood glaring at him, his face swollen and red, his breath coming hard through his nose. He was forty or thereabouts, an unemployed three-hundred-pounder who had grown up dense but happy in his dad's muskrat swamp. School was his hell, and he'd quit at sixteen with the old man's blessing, and then at eighteen his card got drawn and he pulled up his traps and went to Vietnam. It was worse than school. He came home confused in 1971 and resided in the marsh with his dad.

"What's the problem?" Gun said.

Bowser raised a pudgy fist, then dropped it. His thick eyebrows came together in the middle. "You're in your skivs," he said quietly. "I don't want to kick a guy who's in his skivs."

"Just finished my swings and now I'm going for a swim." Gun motioned toward the water. "A few baseballs out there to retrieve. I don't suppose this can wait."

"You don't suppose right," Bowser said. He stood with his big hands curling and uncurling at his sides, apparently uncertain what to say next.

"Okay," Gun said.

Bowser's hands curled into fists and stayed there. "We always liked you, Mr. Pedersen, me and the old man. He used to say you were like us. A guy who wanted to be left alone."

"That's me."

"Not a big shot, even with all your money." Bowser took a step forward. Gun felt tired and cold and wished he had his pants on.

"So I take it kind of hard that you turn on us that way. And the old man, he takes it even harder."

"I didn't turn on you, Bowser. Your dad could've held on to that land."

"Could've held on to it, like hell. Hedman wanted our piece like you wouldn't believe. The old man, he's getting real slow now. You know." Gun didn't know, but he'd heard. Jeremy Devitz had sold out so his only son would have some money after he died, which would probably be soon. He wanted to protect Bowser. Might as well have shot him.

"Bowser, you're welcome to stay and talk this over. If that's to your liking, then let's go in the house and do it over coffee. Otherwise, I think you should go on home."

Gun noticed for the first time that Bowser's eyes looked in two different directions; at the moment, south and southwest.

"I went to see Hedman, see, and he tol' me you're the one I oughta be mad at. He said after he tried buying your land here, you tol' him to go and talk to my dad."

"Not true," said Gun.

"And he said that committee of queer Tig's—Save the Lake or whatever the hell they call it—he said last month they went and asked you to help buy my dad's property. Save it. All they wanted was a lousy loan, but you said no. If you'da done that, Loon Country woulda been history and maybe you and me coulda worked out some deal so I wouldn't have to move."

"Maybe," said Gun. He felt fatigued, too tired to be explaining himself to Bowser Devitz. Or anyone else.

"Fella who'd turn nasty like that to his neighbors

oughta have his ass kicked," Bowser went on. "I'm here to kick yours."

"Come in or go home, Bowser." Gun started past him toward the house.

It took a while to get there. As Gun brushed past him, Bowser turned and funneled his full three hundred pounds into one fist, aimed low. It connected with the pad of unprepared muscle covering Gun's kidney. It pushed the breath from him and made his legs forget to stand. Gun went to his knees.

"Not so damn tough now, are you, Pedersen?" Bowser stood off to Gun's right, living proof of the strength of fat men. "What happened? Gone soft since you quit ball? Only folks you can push around now's a sick old man."

Gun brought air into his body, experimentally, letting it fill his lungs. His kidneys quivered. He felt sorry for Bowser, but it wouldn't do to let this go on.

"I gotta tell you, Pedersen. The old man this morning, he got up early and made a big batch of oatmeal." Bowser was waiting for Gun to get back on his feet. He still looked mad. "A great *big* batch of oatmeal, and I said to him, Geez, Pop, it's just you and me, we're never gonna eat all that."

Gun got up. There were green stains on the knees of his longjohns.

"And Pop says, he's laughing now, he says, It ain't for us, boy, it's for Roxie, she loves it. Roxie! Damn, Pedersen, Roxie was this old sow we raised for ham back before I went over the pond. Pop sold her for butchering while I was over there. I remember the letter." Bowser's big fists came up as he talked; they shook slightly in front of his chest.

Gun's legs were steadier now and his kidneys felt altered but still whole. He said, "Things are that bad."

"Things have been bad for years now. But the sale,

Pedersen, that finished it. Pop blinks his eyes and another ten years is gone. He thinks I'm a high school kid. He thinks Ma's just gone into town."

"Let's go inside," Gun said cautiously.

"Bastard!" said Bowser. His lead blow was a right hand square with Gun's breastbone It filled Gun's lungs with quicksand and he stepped back, twice. Bowser plowed ahead with a windmill left at the solar plexus, but Gun twisted his torso and the blow skipped off. There was a time, Gun realized, when even that first, kidney-burning punch would never have landed; some animal nerve would have warned him, some movement in the air, and his body would have acted without him. Now that nerve seemed dormant, his defensive reflex tired. And Bowser was just winding up.

"Too old for this, are you, Pedersen?" Bowser said. He moved in with another roundhouse. Gun ducked this one and Bowser slipped on the dewy grass, thumping down butt first next to a dismembered old lawn mower Gun had been trying to fix. Bowser struggled up with the ease of a land-bound hippo, his gut plunging. "So you're a ducker," he said. "Shouldn't surprise me. You ducked Loon Country, sure as hell." Bowser moved more carefully now, planting his feet, waving his fists like an old-time boxer. Gun stood with his arms slightly bent in front of him. He told himself to block those fists. No more, and certainly no less. Couldn't blame Bowser for feeling this way, after all. It was just too bad he was so damn strong. Block the fists, Gun told himself, and when the boy's tired he'll go on home.

Fist number one came almost too quick. A left jab, and Gun's right palm barely deflected it in time to save his nose. Come on, Gun thought. You did this enough on the ball field. Bowser threw another jab, and again Gun slapped it away. Another jab missed

Gun's chin by half a foot. Bowser was panting harder now, frustrated that his energy wasn't landing anywhere. A rag of dark hair had flipped down into his eyes and he pushed it back with his knuckles. Gun told him, "You can still quit."

That brought Bowser's fists in again. Gun fouled off the jabs like a pair of bad pitches and let a right fly past his head, carrying Bowser behind it. He saw Bowser slip again, land in a full-faced sprawl this time and lay quiet. He saw Bowser's eyes wishing for some kind of weapon, and he saw them light on the pieces of the old lawn mower a few feet ahead. One piece was a blade.

"Don't do that, Bowser," Gun said, but the big man had already wiggled forward and grabbed the blade. It was a heavy steel rotor that would lay a twenty-four-inch swath when properly sharp, and Bowser's grip on it as he got to his feet turned his whole hand white and then crimson-striped as the edge bit in. He walked toward Gun with the blade drawn back and a mustache of mud under his nose.

"You don't want to do that, Bowser."

Bowser shook his head. A dime-size chunk of mud slid down his chin. "Don't want to. But I'm going to."

Gun said, "Your dad'll be missing you, Bowser." Bowser stood with his feet widespread, his weight bending his legs slightly inward at the knees. Gun walked straight at him until they stood a scant yard from each other. Bowser's eyes were red and watery. Blood ran from his fingers where he gripped the blade. It ran down his upraised forearm and dripped from his elbow.

"Swing if you have to," Gun said.

Bowser swung, a simple level cut that whistled through the air neck high. Gun's hand leaped almost before he knew it, catching Bowser's thick wrist exactly where it joined thumb and pad, stopping the blade, backing it up. Gun tightened his hold on Bowser's wrist and looked into his face. He saw that while Bowser was facing him directly, the paths of his eyes took him off to both sides, left and right. Gun made a fist of his free hand and sent it swiftly to the center, and Bowser fell like stockyard beef to the grass.

Gun left him there and went inside. He made coffee from a red can, boiling it severely on the stove. He had a cup himself and then, still in his longjohns, took the pot outside and set it with a mug next to the silent Bowser.

The morning was still, and a white mist rose up from the lake's unrippled surface like smoke from a cooling battlefield. Gun entered the frigid water without hesitating. He swam forty yards out and dove. The cold ignited a brilliant explosion inside his brain, and he could feel his skin tightening around his muscles like a rubber wetsuit. It was the middle of May, and the lake had been ice-free for only a few weeks.

Ten feet down, at the sandy bottom, Gun opened his eyes. No walleyes here this morning, no streaks of silver heading for deeper waters. Only refracted spears of light entering from above, penetrating the green haze, dissolving like crystals of salt. He looked around but could not find any of the baseballs. He'd waited too long. He kicked for the top.

When he came back in, the lawn and coffeepot were empty, the mug swaying neatly by its handle on the branch of a reaching fir.

2

Gun was on the last phase of his morning workout—
push-ups on his fists against the hard kitchen floor—
when his second visitor of the day arrived. This time
in a pinging, four-cylinder foreign job with squeaky
shocks.

As usual, Mazy shut off the engine and waited for
Gun to come outside. He took his sweet time, slowing
down the push-ups until they hurt.

Mazy had turned fifteen the week her mother died.
Fifteen and needing more from a father than he
thought he could give. He'd tried to explain to her that
he was afraid, that a ballplayer gone from home seven
months a year never learned to be parent enough,
never had time, but she knew it all and said it didn't
matter. She'd stay, she'd be good, she'd cook and do
her homework and keep it all together. Then the aunt
in Wisconsin gave Gun what he thought was a better
option. She opened those big farmhouse doors for the
poor motherless Mazy, and he shoved her right
through, insisting to the last that this was the responsi-

ble thing to do. Mazy had ignored the practical, fluttering aunt and said to Gun as he left her, Don't call it responsible. Call it desertion.

Mazy was usually right. It was a troublesome thing.

Now she sat in her dented MG, half frowning at him behind green aviator-style sunglasses. Her thick red-blond hair was chopped off straight at the jawline and her full wide lips were the same shape as her mother's had been, only set harder. She wore a blue chambray work shirt, collar open at the neck, sleeves rolled to the elbows, and the sun was lighting up the silvery hair on her forearms. It stood straight out from her tanned skin, as though electrified.

"You're even starting to look like a journalist," Gun said. "Here for an interview?"

His daughter looked off toward the water. Not a single muscle moved in her face. "If I were here for an interview, you wouldn't be grinning down at me like that."

"Guess you're right."

"Burger's got a few good stories about you. Sportswriter's nightmare, the way he tells it. 'Forget the crowbar and you'd never get his mouth open.'"

Gun laughed, but Mazy's smile was humorless. And he couldn't tell what her eyes were doing behind those green glasses. "I'll tell him hello for you," she said.

"You do that."

Mazy was twenty-five, and Gun had seen little of her since she turned eighteen. She had gone off to a college in Oregon, then worked for a newspaper in Portland for a couple years before taking the *Tribune* job in Minneapolis. It was good to have her back in the state, but the truth was, she didn't come up to see him very often. Not that he blamed her.

He leaned against the car and took a good lungful of

fresh air, tapped a little rhythm on the tight canvas top of the convertible. When the clench in his chest had loosened enough he said, "Come in for breakfast. I'll take my shower and then we can fry up some eggs and bacon. Got some of that good stuff from Harold at the locker. How about it?"

"You know what I'm here about, Dad . . ."

"Oh, come on." He yanked opened her door and offered a hand, held the other behind his back in a gesture of mock courtesy. Groaning, she took hold of his fingers. He pulled her to her feet. "That's my girl."

"God," groaned Mazy.

Showering, he pictured his daughter moving about in the bright pine kitchen, cracking eggs and brewing coffee, setting the table with Amanda's old china. He knew perfectly well why she was here. In fact he was surprised she hadn't come sooner.

Already six months had gone by since Gun had signed his property over to Mazy—all four hundred acres of it, including a quarter-mile of prime lakeshore. At the time Loon Country had been little more than a rumor. Still, the phone calls from Lyle Hedman and Tig Larson, the county commissioner, made Gun angry. He'd asked himself, What's a clean, simple way of staying out of things? What do you have to do to make people leave you the hell alone, once and for all? The answer came back. The best thing to do is, you leave.

He told his daughter he wanted to beat the state's inheritance laws. If he should happen to die before his time, she shouldn't have to spend years in the purgatory of probate courts. That's what he told her. Reluctantly, she agreed to go along with the idea. She didn't know about Loon Country yet, or not much.

Gun had his lawyer fix it all up. Mazy got the land

for a lot less than market value, and Gun financed the sale himself. Nothing to it—except from the beginning he knew that sooner or later Mazy would figure out what he was up to.

Now the time had come, and she had one more thing to hold against him.

3

He walked barefoot into the kitchen, making wet footprints on the linoleum. A wide skylight was cut into the high vaulted ceiling, and beneath it his daughter had breakfast going. Bacon sputtered on the big round cast-iron griddle, and eggs sizzled in a copper-bottomed pan. She didn't say a word as he sat down at the table.

She handed him a fully-loaded plate: oven-baked hash browns, three eggs sunny-side up, four strips of thick bacon from the Stony locker, a piece of toast. He got up and went to the stove and poured two cups of coffee from the enamel pot.

They sat down. Mazy looked at him evenly from across the table, her lips turned up in a hard smile. Gun took a large gulp of coffee and said, "I hear you've been in town for a while, working."

Mazy nodded at him.

"And house-sitting for that new editor of the local booster sheet."

"The *Journal*'s not a booster sheet. Not anymore. Have you bothered to take a look at it since Carol took over?"

Gun shook his head.

"And how do you know where I'm staying? Got your buddy Jack spying on me, or what?"

"Look. Honey. Wouldn't it be a little strange if Jack talked to you and then saw me and didn't tell me what he knew? The guy's my friend. You're my daughter." He shrugged.

She took off her sunglasses and lay them beside her plate. Her brown eyes were tired-looking, bloodshot, and for the first time ever Gun noticed wrinkles in the soft skin underneath.

"Yeah, okay," she said. "I'm sorry."

"I am too. I should have told you."

Mazy straightened up. A mean sparkle lit up her eyes. "That's right—and I would've talked you out of it. Maybe you need a buffer between you and the cruel world out there"—she flung her fingers toward the door—"but it doesn't have to be me. And I don't like being lied to, either."

"I didn't lie to you, Mazy."

"You just avoided telling me ninety-five percent of the truth."

Gun looked away, then down at his hands. He said, "You can do whatever you want with the land. I'm not asking you to protect it. You can keep it forever, or you can sell out to Lyle for a million bucks and let him build a giant waterslide on it. It's up to you. I don't want anybody fighting my battles. All I want is to be left alone. I want to find a place up north as quiet as this place used to be. I want to live up there, and I want people to let me be."

"So that you're able to continue your penance," Mazy said. "Am I supposed to be impressed?"

Gun shook his head. "Nope."

"Good. Because I'm sick and tired of your guilty pride, or whatever it is that keeps you out here in the woods." She spit the words at him.

Gun lifted his eyes to his daughter's face, flexed the muscles of his jaw and leveled a finger at her. He dropped his voice a register. "You know what you'd be saying if I'd decided to stay here and use my influence to try and kill this Loon Country thing? If I *did* get involved, you know what you'd say?"

"No, what would I say?"

"You'd be all over me for throwing my weight around. You'd say I hadn't changed after all. You'd come up with every argument under the sun to prove that Lyle Hedman's project is good for the area, good for the people around here. You'd make the guy out to be some kind of philanthropist." Gun laughed and took a bite of toast with egg on it. "Tell me I'm wrong," he said, aiming his fork at her, chewing.

"Maybe I would," said Mazy.

"You would."

She took a deep breath and let it out slowly, opened her lips as if to speak, then clamped them shut again. She shook her head and turned her attention to breakfast.

When she was finished eating, she arranged her silverware neatly on her plate—it was something she'd done ever since Gun could remember—and put her green sunglasses back on. "None of it makes the least bit of difference," she said. "You know that."

"What do you mean?"

"To Mom," said Mazy. "Or to me, for that matter."

"Makes a difference to me, though." He stood up and quickly cleared the table, started filling the sink with hot water. Mazy stayed where she was.

As he'd done thousands of times in the last ten years, Gun forced a scene into his mind—it was a formalized nightmare now, one he used against himself for reasons he left alone: Amanda, home from work and wrapped in a towel, is running her bathwater. She hears the phone and picks it up, expecting Gun's voice, reassurance that the rumors are just rumors. But it's another man's voice. He's a reporter, he says, *American Mirror*. He asks what she feels like, sharing her star.

Two or three times in his career Gun had seen his face on the tabloids. It had always been laughable stuff: Gun Pedersen's Magic Bat. It got him kidded in the clubhouse, but all this about Susannah . . . He'd never spoken to the woman again; it made him sick to think of his own success and the endless goddamn choices that had come with it.

That evening Amanda boarded a flight for Minneapolis, where the Tigers were playing the Twins. She was coming, she told Gun—phoning him after the reporter's call—to straighten things out finally. But she never arrived. Her plane went down in a farmer's cornfield west of Eau Claire.

Now he shut off the water and pushed the sleeves of his sweatshirt up past his elbows. He took a clean dishrag from the wooden peg above the sink and submerged a handful of silverware in the suds. Mazy got up from the table and went to the refrigerator, where a stained white towel hung from the door handle.

"People are saying all kinds of things," Gun said. "You've probably heard most of it already."

"Probably."

"How I'm ducking a fight, siding with the big-money boys, selling out the environmentalists." He rinsed a fistful of silverware and set it carefully in the drain rack.

"Well, the truth is you *could* have done something. People around here would've listened to you. You've been here awhile now, you've got money. If you had wanted, you could've bought the Devitz land yourself —like that committee of Tig's asked you to. You could have pulled it right out from under Lyle Hedman's feet. People know that. No land, no Loon Country."

"Jeremy needs every cent he can get out of that swamp of his," said Gun. "Lyle gave him top dollar."

"Jeremy would've let it go for half the price to save this lake."

"And then Lyle would have gone after someone else's land and people would've asked me to buy that too."

"Maybe."

Out the window above the sink Gun watched a high range of mountain-blue clouds advance from the west and put a hard slate surface on the water. He was nearly finished washing the dishes when Mazy spoke again. "Are you going to the benefit tonight?"

"What's that?"

"The Hedmans are throwing a dinner and dance, proceeds to the paper-mill workers who've been laid off."

"Yeah? Pretty funny, considering Hedmans laid them off. Great P.R. stunt. The man of means who cares about the little guy."

"It was Geoff's idea."

"Good for Geoff. He must've inherited the old man's sense of humor."

"Geoff has . . . changed," said Mazy. Something shifted in her voice.

"And Jack tells me you've been spending quite a little time with him this week." Gun hadn't meant to bring it up but he couldn't help it.

She turned and stared at him, hard. "I don't think that's any of your concern."

He lifted both hands out of the water and held

them, palms out, in front of his chest. "All right, okay."

She dried a plate, twisting her neck around like she did when she was trying to relax. "What I was wondering is, how about going with me tonight? Somebody wants to meet you."

"I've already met Geoff, remember?" Gun tried to put a look on his face that said, All in good fun. "I'm sure *he* does."

Mazy sighed. "No. Carol Long. She's getting back into town tonight."

He shook his head. "Sorry. I'm driving north this afternoon to look at some land. Won't be back until late."

"Fine, then." She dropped her towel on the counter and walked to the door. As she swung open the screen, Gun spoke her name. She stopped on the threshold and turned. Her face was inscrutable. He tried to smile at her but couldn't.

"Just tell me there's nothing between you and Geoff," he said. "He's not worth your time. Tell me you're only using him to get at the story."

Mazy worked her hands into the tight front pockets of her Levi's jeans. "I'm only using him to get at the story," she said, then she left and the door slammed behind her.

Standing at the sink, soapy wet hands hanging down at his sides, Gun watched his daughter walk toward her car. The sway in her stride was the same as her mother's had been, and she held her head cocked a little to the right, as if listening to a quiet voice. It was a habit of hers since she was a small girl and suffered damage to her hearing from an ear infection.

She started her car now, turned it around, and drove out of sight around the bend in Gun's rutted driveway. He realized his phone was ringing.

4

He picked it up and said, "Hmm."

"Gun—God, I'm glad you're there!"

"Who is this? Tig? You don't sound so good."

"I'm awful, could you please—" His voice broke into a cough and he grabbed a breath that sounded like a straw sucking the bottom of a glass.

"Maybe if you'd quit those long brown cigarettes of yours."

"Gun, you've gotta get over here."

"What's going on?"

"You'll understand when you get here. Please." The receiver clicked and he was gone.

"I'm on my way, Tig," said Gun, smiling.

Tig Larson, the county commissioner, was a man who treated life itself as an emergency, so Gun didn't feel the need to hurry. He walked out to his Ford pickup, a white '71 F-150 sitting by the garage. Its windshield, victim of a wicked foul ball, looked like a road map of New York. When Gun turned the key, the engine backfired once, then started up in a ragged rhythm that shook the cab. He waited for the eight cylinders to find their balance, then turned a circle around home plate and followed his daughter's tracks.

Tig lived on the other side of the lake in a disgusting little cluster of suburban-type homes, and Gun took the long way around instead of going through town. He followed the narrow lake road and drove with his window down, enjoying the cool breeze off the water.

Most likely the commissioner had worked himself into a state of nerves thinking about the referendum next week. He was probably out to make a last ditch effort to enlist Gun's help. It wouldn't be hard to turn him down. Tig wasn't the sort that evoked much sympathy in Gun. A big, soft-bodied, effeminate man, Tig was the subject of rumors Gun believed were probably true. Which didn't help his cause a whole lot. Up here, people were reluctant to rally around a man of Tig's reputed sexual preference, even people who respected him for his stand on the environment.

His home was small and neat and built into the south side of a man-made hill, and this morning he had pulled the dark shades over the floor-to-ceiling windows that covered his front-facing wall. Gun knocked and Tig opened the door just a crack, peered out at him over the chain of the safety lock.

"You look a little under the weather," Gun said. It was true. The man's heavy face was fish-belly white.

Tig groaned his relief. "Thanks for coming." He opened the door and let Gun in. "Here, I'll get us a drink first," he said, reaching for a bottle that sat on the big console television.

"First?" said Gun. "No thanks."

Tig poured himself half a tumbler of brandy and drank it straight off.

"What's going on, anyway?"

Blinking away the sting, Tig pointed a trembling finger outside. When he could talk again, he told Gun to follow him, then led the way out the door and down the slope twenty yards to a small wooden storage shed. He stopped a few feet short of it and wiped at his eyes with the knuckles of both hands. "It's in there," he said.

Gun stepped up to the building and went inside. There weren't any windows and it was too black to see anything, but he could smell something unhealthy in the close air. "You got a light in here?"

"On the wall to your right."

Gun flicked the switch and looked around, found himself staring into the wide, scared, bloody eyes of a cat. A yellow tabby. It blinked twice, then made a sound like a child clearing its throat. "Hoo," Gun breathed. The cat was spread out wide and staked against the wall, nails driven through all four paws. It was sliced open from throat to anus, and loops of multicolored entrails hung clear to the floor.

"Still alive," Tig moaned from outside.

Gun stepped from the shed, thinking of himself at thirteen, having to shoot his big Newfoundland dog Sally after she got hit on the road by the mailman's car. He'd used the twelve-gauge at close range, quick and precise, and hadn't cried until he dragged her off into the woods for burial and felt the dead weight of her. Now he walked past Tig to the pickup truck, took the .38 Smith & Wesson from underneath the seat and came back.

"Oh, my God," said Tig. Gun rested a hand briefly on the man's shoulder, then reentered the shed.

He was careful to plug one ear with a finger and turn the other away from the pistol, but the shot was still incredibly loud inside the small building. The cat relaxed and its head drooped forward. There was a small new hole of sky in the wall. Gun found a hammer and removed the nails. He took the animal down and buried it off in the scrub weeds beyond Tig's lawn.

"I don't think you're listening, Gun. My God, it's terrorism, plain and simple, can't you see it? Hedman's trying to turn me around, mess up my head. The man's paranoid. He's got all the money, he's got the support of almost everybody with any real influence around here, and he's still afraid he's gonna lose. He's been out here to visit me half a dozen times in the last month. Trying to get me to change my mind. And the last time he got mad. Made some threats."

"Such as."

"I can't go into it, Gun. Simply can't." Tig's round shoulders rose and fell dramatically.

"So what are you asking me to do?" Gun shook his head as Tig offered him the bottle, watched as the man refilled his own glass yet again.

"Aw, damn, I don't know. It's getting pretty late in the game to do anything. Would have been nice, though, if there was somebody else on my side to take a little of the heat, you know? Somebody like you. Used to think of you as a friend. Or at least a guy who wouldn't back down when somebody wanted to shit in his water." Tig sniffed. "That money you gave to Walleyes Unlimited. Really helped. And the time you caught those poachers north of old man Young's place." Tig's voice was getting whiny, sloppy. "I thought you were the sort of guy that comes through in a jam. Not somebody who runs off, you know?"

Gun got up to leave. "Sorry, but I can't do anything. You'll have to handle it alone, Tig."

"You wanna see Hedman win this one, that's what I think. You stand to make a little cash on the deal, don'tcha?"

Gun leaned down over the man and put a finger into his soft chest. Tig scooted his chair backward. "Look," Gun said. "I think this plan of Hedman's stinks, okay? Same as you do. But there's a lot of folks around here, and I mean a lot of them, who don't happen to agree with us."

"Who? Tell me who?"

Gun sat back down at the table and propped up the elbow of his talking arm, took a breath. "The guy laid off from Hedman's mill, say. Got a bunch of kids at home and his wife's out waiting on tables or serving drinks." He had to stop to fight off a rush of shame in his belly. He'd never been a bullshitter and it was too late to start now.

Tig laughed drunkenly. "You'd make a lousy politician, know that?"

Gun got to his feet again and moved toward the door. "That's right. You've got plenty of those types running around already. Let them fight it out. People like yourself and Reverend Barr. You guys can summon your forces and have your little war and one side'll win. That's how these things work. I don't want any part of it."

Tig drained off another glass of brandy and laughed again, bitterly, shaking his head. "I've heard people say this before about you, Gun, but up till now I never wanted to believe it."

"What's that?"

"You don't know the meaning of loyalty. You watch out for the big slugger, numero uno, and to hell with the rest of the crowd. Guess your wife could have said something about that, huh?"

Gun felt like a man who's been dealt a punishing blow to the gut. He took a deep breath and blew it out, turned and opened the door. "Yeah, I guess you're right. She could at that." He nodded and left.

That afternoon he drove north as he had planned,

but the property he was thinking of buying didn't look nearly as good this time. Partly it was the rain that had moved in. It came down hard and steady and smelled like fish. The air was still, not a trace of wind, and everywhere Gun looked he saw the same miserable gray concoction of heavy weather he was feeling inside.

He missed his appointment with the realtor on purpose and drove on home. That night he went to bed early and dreamed about things he couldn't remember the next morning. All he knew was he hadn't gotten much rest. He had to unwrap himself from the twisted bedsheets.

5

Next morning. Cool sun. Gun was toweling down after his swim, dripping all over the kitchen floor, when someone rapped three quick beats on the door.

"Come in."

"Mr. Pedersen?" The door opened and a woman stepped in, no one he knew. She wore black jeans, long ones, and black pumps that bared tan ankles to the chill of morning. She had black bangs with a few gray strands scattered over her forehead, and lake-green eyes Gun found himself wanting to look good for.

"Sorry about the longjohns," he said.

She smiled, an easy tropical smile, then turned it down some and said, "I'm Carol Long, the new editor of the *Stony Journal.* Your daughter's been watching my place for me."

"Yes." Gun shoved his wet hair back with his fingers, and a cold cup of Stony Lake ran down his spine. He looked at Carol Long's relentless legs and attempted rational thought. "Yes. Mazy's mentioned you. You met at that reporters' thing in Minneapolis."

"The symposium, right." The smile left and a little fluster came into her voice. "Mazy's not here."

"She should be?"

"I was hoping so. I couldn't get back last night, so I called her, asked her to stay on an extra day. I pulled in half an hour ago, and she's gone. Thought she might be over here."

Gun finished with the towel and pointed to the stove. "There's coffee. Mind if I put some clothes on?"

"If you must." The smile made a fleeting comeback.

He went to the bedroom and wondered what she was doing, coming out here like this. Not even eight in the morning. Must be something important if she was in such a hurry to find Mazy. There were nerves in her voice. Nothing nervous about the way she moved, though, Sweet Heaven no. Gun wondered if she knew how she looked to him; those slim black jeans, that smile, probably she did. He wondered how he looked to her, a man edging past the middle years, in goosebumps and soaking longies. Hair still thick but going white before its time. He shut it from his mind and found gray wool socks, jeans, a red wool shirt. It was cool in the house, even with Carol Long there.

She was at the kitchen table ignoring a cup of coffee and nibbling discreetly at a silver-set emerald on her left hand. Gun poured and sat down.

"Now," he smiled, "what's so important you've got to come chasing my girl before breakfast gets cold?"

"Mr. Pedersen, it's not that. Listen. She was supposed to stay at my house through today. We talked about it. Now I drive in, early, she's nowhere in sight. There's her typewriter, even some notes lying next to it, a blank sheet rolled in. Her car's in the drive. But she's not there."

"She runs in the mornings sometimes," Gun said. "Two, three miles, farther once in a while."

Carol Long cleared her throat. Her eyes met Gun's and he saw a spark of steel in them. "Mr. Pedersen. Do you know why I wanted someone in my house while I was gone?"

"It's Gun. No, I don't."

"I've had some trouble with vandals. And I was threatened."

"It's a virus around here lately," Gun said. "Go on."

"So far just a few well-chosen words spray-painted across my picture window, but I got a phone call promising worse. I suppose you can guess what it's about."

"Mmm. I could."

"You do read the *Journal,* I suppose."

"I'm sure it's a good paper," said Gun.

Carol stiffened, then said, "I've been running editorials against the Loon Country development."

"Mr. Lyle Hedman wouldn't appreciate that." Gun lifted his coffee, looked at Carol over the cup. "Did Mazy know why you wanted somebody at your place?"

"Of course. Look, she's been poking around enough to get some people upset. Good reporters do that. I just thought . . ." She let the sentence die on the table.

"You think she got somebody upset enough to do something damn stupid," Gun said. "All right. Let's be sensible. You say her car's still there, her typewriter. What about her other stuff, clothes and things?"

Carol looked at Gun, red coming up under her tan. "God, I didn't even look, I didn't think. I'm sorry, it just seemed so weird and empty in the house, that old IBM of hers humming on the table all by itself—I came straight out. I thought maybe you'd picked her up, spur of the moment, go get some breakfast, I don't know." She stood abruptly and went to the door. Gun followed.

"I live twenty minutes from here. I'll call you." Carol smoothed her hair, showed emerald ring, green eyes.

"She'll probably be there waiting for you," Gun said. "Don't worry, Mrs. Long."

"Not Mrs.," Carol said, and went.

Gun went back to the kitchen, opened a drawer and removed a narrow red can of tobacco and a matchbook of papers. He quickly rolled a cigarette, lit it, then sat down at the table to smoke. The clock above the old round-top refrigerator said quarter of eight. Between drags Gun twirled the cigarette like a baton in his big fingers and blew smoke rings up toward the open-beam ceiling. He told himself his daughter knew how to take care of herself, that she wasn't a kid any longer, that she was subtle enough and smart enough to keep people from feeling threatened. She knew how to put folks at ease, unlike most journalists Gun had known. And he'd known far too many. Anyway, she was probably just out running.

The phone rang and Gun picked it up. "Hello."

"Carol Long." Now her voice was low and controlled. "I checked in the bathroom, and her makeup and toothpaste and cosmetic case, it's all there. But it's strange. I looked in the bedroom, in the dresser and closet. Most of her clothes are gone, underwear, socks, jeans, all six pairs of them—I was talking to her when she unpacked. Her suitcase too. She shoved that under the bed, and it's not there now. Mr. Pedersen, Mazy left in a hurry. I think you'd better call the police."

Gun shifted the receiver from one ear to the other and started rolling a new cigarette. "Carol, didn't Mazy tell me you've been a reporter in Hawaii for the last twenty years or so?"

"That's right."

"I suppose over there people call the cops when they think someone's in trouble. Here in Stony it's not that simple."

"Oh?"

"How well are you acquainted with the police here—Chief Bunn?"

Gun waited while Carol drew a slow breath. "He seems . . . competent enough."

"Really?"

"Yes." Firm now.

Gun put the unlit cigarette between his lips, took his time, reached for a kitchen match. "Carol, I shouldn't, but I'm going to tell you a story. True one." He scratched the match on the black burner of the stove. He lit the cigarette and waved the match out. "You know Harley Arnold, the grocer."

"Sure."

"He's a neighbor of Bunn's half a mile or so down the road. A few winters ago now he caught a couple fool kids from the high school swiping cooking sherry from his shelves. He called their folks. Couple nights later somebody drove past his house and put half a dozen .22 slugs in his cedar siding."

Carol was quiet.

"So Arnold called Bunn, and Bunn came over the next night to see if anyone would try it again. He parked the police car behind a big snowdrift a block from Arnold's, and he waited in Arnold's junipers for three hours, pistol in hand."

"Okay."

"Okay. But while he was waiting, those same fool kids came along and took the police car for a ride. Parked it in some frozen rushes out on the lake. He'd left the keys in it."

"All right, pretty stupid. But at least he gave it a try. He could've done worse."

"He did worse. At eleven o'clock he said good night to Arnold and went on home. But he walked home. Forgot he'd ever brought the car. He didn't notice it was gone until the next morning, and it was a week before anyone found it." Gun tapped ashes into the sink. "There's nothing bad about Chief Bunn, Carol. He just ought not to be a cop."

"I see." Carol paused. "What about Sheriff Bakke? Have you got a reason not to call him?"

Gun smiled. "You probably don't have time for another story. And I don't have time to tell it."

"So. You're going to take care of this yourself."

"That's right. Good-bye, now, and thanks for the call." He hung up, finished dressing, went outside and started his truck. He didn't hurry. Between his heart and stomach he could feel something cool and hard and buoyant, like an icy balloon. It was a familiar feeling, and an old one. During his seventeen years with the Tigers he'd had it often, usually in the late innings when he came to bat with men on base. A good number of his 426 home runs had floated out on the icy balloon. Gun thought of it as a gathering place of his energy, concentration, and nerve. It put his brain on automatic, sharpened his senses. Since leaving the game ten years ago, though, the feeling had been absent. Now it was back, and Gun was grateful for its return.

6

He went south on the lake road and headed into town. Stony, population 3415 according to the green sign at the edge of town, stood on the southern bank of Stony Lake. The year-round people lived in modest wood-frame houses, and most of them worked at the Hedman Paper Mill twelve miles to the east. The rest lived off the tourist trade in the summer and collected unemployment checks all winter.

Two miles out of town he stopped at a small tavern nearly hidden by a dense stand of birches. Behind it the lake glittered. A neon sign blinked from a window, bright green: JACK BE NIMBLE'S. Gun parked in the lot and walked inside. The walls were knotty pine, darkly golden in the weak light.

Behind the gleaming mahogany bar stood a man in a black crew cut. He was short and looked like a rough bust of a Roman patrician, stoic, not a soft feature in his face. On the wall behind him hung a lighted glass shadow box with a pear-shaped bear paddling a canoe on a brilliant blue lake. In the sky above the bear, clouds spelled out the words Hamm's Beer.

"Earlier than usual."

"I came to talk, Jack, not patronize."

"You still gotta pay." Jack set a cup of black coffee on the bar. "Twins beat your Tigers, see that? Ten-five."

"With a staff ERA pushing five they *better* keep hitting."

"Sour grapes. You're a sore loser, Gun."

"You seen Mazy the last couple days?" Gun asked.

"Let me think," said Jack, drumming his fingers on the bar. "Yeah, day before yesterday, in the evening. About seven-thirty."

"Alone was she?"

Jack opened his mouth, froze for an instant, then shook his head. "Geoff," he said.

Gun stared ahead into the mirror behind Jack's assortment of bottles and didn't like what he saw. His eyes, dark above the high cliffs of his cheekbones, made him look like a man older than himself, a man not quite in control of his faculties. He felt a stab of anger in his chest, and to stifle it he squeezed the heavy mug of coffee in his hands. Something snapped. He looked down at the mug, in two clean halves now. Coffee spread on the ebony bar. He opened his fingers—they hadn't been cut—and let his friend take away the broken pieces.

Jack mopped up the coffee with a towel, replaced the cup with a new one, and leaned forward, resting his forearms on the bar. "Let's hear about it," he said.

"Mazy's gone." Gun told him about Carol's visit, and when he'd finished, pressed his palms together, matching finger for finger. "It just looks bad," he said.

Jack wiped at a spot on the bar with a rag, squinting. "Damnit, Gun, I didn't think much of it, Mazy and Geoff together. Just figured she was getting her story together for the paper, pumping him for the inside stuff."

"I'm sure she was. But how did she seem? You know her. Was she in control?"

Jack pointed across the room, behind Gun. "They were in that booth there. Hedman looked pretty eager, sat up straight as a little pup. Bought some nice wine, the most expensive stuff I keep. I saw him reach for her hand a couple times, that sort of thing."

"And Mazy?"

Jack shook his head. "Friendly enough to keep him talking, cool enough to keep him honest, is how it looked to me. Gun"—Jack lifted a blunt finger—"if I'd thought for a second that she was having any trouble with him, I'd have broken his ass."

"I know," Gun said.

"I figured Mazy knew what she was up to. Didn't want to put the chill on her interview. Damn. I'm sorry, Gun."

"Don't worry, I'm sure everything's fine." Gun shifted on his stool and tapped his white coffee cup on the bar. "Think I'll take a little drive out to skinny Lyle's place. It's been too long—let's see, about nine years since I was out there." Gun winked.

"Don't be so hard on him this time."

Gun finished the last of his coffee and got to his feet. "I won't," he said, starting for the door.

"You need any help and you know where to look," Jack said.

It was the year after the accident, Mazy sixteen and spending the summer with Gun, that he paid his first visit to Lyle Hedman. That particular August night Mazy was having a party in the woods north of the house. Gun had put up a big canvas Army tent for the girls to sleep in.

At one in the morning Gun woke to screams,

high-pitched girl screams that he could feel between his ears like razor-sharp wires, stretched and shivering. He pulled on his pants and ran outside. The night was warm and clear and the sky shimmered with heat lightning. The tent was several hundred yards north of the house, and Gun was almost there when he saw a flash of movement in the trees. He flattened himself belly to ground and scuttled forward.

The tent was pitched in a clearing the size of a softball diamond, and Gun stopped at the edge of it. There were no sounds coming from the tent, no one moving inside it. Then a shout came from Gun's left and three young men in swim trunks and Halloween masks charged from the trees. They ran straight for the tent, throwing what looked like tomatoes or apples as they came. The missiles thumped the canvas. The girls inside screamed. One of the boys yelled, "Sharon's turn!" and all three of them pushed through the tent's canvas doorway. After a few seconds of scuffling, the boys emerged with one of the girls, Sharon Turner, whose voice rose like an ambulance siren, so high and piercing Gun could almost see it. She was overweight and wore white pajamas, and the boys had her by the arms and legs, her bottom dragging on the ground.

"Hey, Geoff!" This from a boy wearing a rubber Frankenstein mask who flicked on a high-intensity flashlight and aimed it toward the trees. Like magic, a naked body appeared, jumping, twisting, and goose-stepping over the grass. The streaker wore a Jimmy Carter mask and headed for the tent and the shrieking girl, veering off only at the last instant and disappearing into the trees.

Gun stood and sprinted for the boys, who were laughing and still holding onto Sharon Turner. When they saw him they dropped her and ran. He knew where they had most likely parked, and when he was sure the girls were all right, he set off for the dead-end gravel driveway. He followed the shortest possible route, sliding down a twenty-foot embankment then fording a narrow stream, and intercepted the boys just before they reached their car. Three of them fled on foot, but Gun managed to hang onto the fourth, grinning Jimmy Carter, and tore away the mask. It was Geoff Hedman, twenty-year-old son of Lyle. The car parked on the dead-end drive was his—a new Jaguar. Gun found the keys in the ignition and told Geoff to get in, he'd drive him home. Geoff scrambled into the backseat, his head down, and shucked into his clothes.

Hedman's main house was a painstaking copy of an African hunting lodge. From its low-hanging eaves the roof extended steeply to a high peak and was thatched with long yellow grasses imported from Kenya. Lining the drive were gas torches mounted on bleached wooden poles carved to resemble large bones. That night the torches were all lit, and the flames wavered in the breeze off the lake. The windows of the lodge blazed. Cars were parked bumper to bumper along the drive.

Gun pulled up beneath a flickering lamp. He spoke for the first time since he had started the car. "As soon as you do one thing, Geoff, we'll go into the house."

"I swear, Mr. Pedersen, it wasn't my idea. I didn't want to do it. I'm sorry, I really am." Geoff had been apologizing nonstop for fifteen minutes. "We were just out for some fun, trying to scare them a little."

"You scared them, all right," Gun said. "Now you're going to have some real fun. What you do, you take those clothes of yours back off. Then we're going in."

"What?" Geoff's eyes watered in surprise. He shook his head quickly.

"You heard me."

"No," said Geoff.

Gun reached back over the seat and slapped the young man across the cheek. Geoff started to cry. But he took his clothes off.

Without knocking, Gun opened the door of Hedman's lodge, thrust Geoff inside, then walked in himself. He stood on a woven cane welcome mat and gripped a pinkly naked Geoff by the upper arm. Geoff tried to crouch and cover himself, but Gun held him up straight. The party was loud and animated. In the center of the room a stuffed African elephant was frozen in what appeared to be mid-beller, tusks lifted toward the ceiling. Beneath the elephant Hedman and his wife held court from the seat of a leather couch, nodding and smiling at a pressing cluster of guests. Throughout the big room groups of people formed intimate knots, arms draped around each other, heads moving agreeably with drink. For a full thirty seconds no one noticed Gun and Geoff. Then Hedman's eyes wandered toward the door, flashed, and widened. His wife, then the people near him, and finally the whole crowd, turned to stare. The room drained of every sound. In the silence Geoff moaned.

Then Gun spoke quietly. "Lyle, your kid's been on my property. When all your friends have gone home, you better ask him what he was doing there."

Hedman opened his mouth but nothing came out. Gun let go of Geoff's arm and left the house. He drove the Jaguar into town and walked the five miles home from there.

7

Now Gun was on his way to visit Hedman for a second time, first time in daylight. He turned off the lake road about six miles northeast of Stony, at a black sign shaped like an elephant with tusks lifted. The white letters of the sign said KENYA DRIVE—PRIVATE. A hundred yards in, a gate with iron bars blocked the drive. Gun stopped his truck and got out. The gate hadn't been here nine years ago. Neither had the twelve-foot-high chain-link fence that reached away in both directions, sealing off Hedman's property. Maybe Lyle was as paranoid as Tig said he was.

On the other side of the gate stood a young man wearing an orange sleeveless jumpsuit—probably sleeveless because the man's upper arms were too big to fit inside a shirt. Gun estimated his height at five-ten, his weight at 230. He had the kind of body Gun had noticed on lots of young men recently, bulky and smooth and designed for the rather limited task of moving heavy barbells up and down. At the man's side was a .38 in a holster with a safety strap.

As Gun walked toward the gate, he took from his trouser pocket a receipt for two hundred-pound bags of cement he'd purchased from Darwin's Lumber in Stony. He folded the receipt twice.

"Hello," said Gun.

"You call ahead?" asked the guard.

"No reservation, sorry."

"Then I guess you're out of luck. Hedman doesn't have time for walk-ins."

"Fine. I'll just give you a note for him." Gun moved up to the iron gate, reached his hand through the bars and offered the folded receipt. "Make sure he gets it," he said.

The guard's fingers touched the receipt, and quick as a northern pike slamming a spoon, Gun seized the man's wrist, yanked him off his feet, and pulled him hard against the bars. The man's head knocked the iron like a block of wood. Gun let go of the wrist, took a handful of hair, and maintaining a steady pull on the guy's head, he reached between the bars with his free hand. He unsnapped the holster strap, palmed the gun, and let the man go.

The guard fell backward on his rear end, cradling the top of his head in his elbows. His eyes were clamped shut and he cursed in violent whispers, like a young boy trying valiantly not to cry.

"Open the gate," Gun said, "or I'll have to pop one of those high-protein biceps."

Rubbing his crown with one hand, the guard shoved himself up to his knees. He sorted through the big circle of keys hanging from his belt and opened the lock.

Gun swung the gate open wide. "Now," he said, "if you want to look like a monkey in front of your boss, you can come with me. If not, start running toward Stony. It's that way." He pointed.

The orange-suited guard glanced up briefly at Gun, then rose unsteadily to his feet and began trotting toward the road.

"I said running," Gun called out, and the guard picked up his pace.

The winding drive cut through a forest of mature white aspen, then up a steep hill onto a small field of grass and wild daisies. Finally it tunneled straight into the deep shade of a thick pine woods before breaking through into a clearing of manicured lawn. Once more Gun saw the huge lodge, its thatched roof twitching in the strong breeze like the stiff hair on a dog's back. Beyond it was Stony Lake, choppy today, blue-black waves capped with gray foam. He parked the truck and was about to walk to the front door when he saw Hedman down on the long floating dock. He was stowing gear on one of his boats and didn't look up until Gun stepped onto the dock, rocking it slightly.

Hedman finished tightening the cap on a red fuel tank and smiled without adjusting the muscles of his face. All that happened was the thin line of his mouth lengthened insignificantly. "Hello, Gun," Hedman said. He picked up the tank and stepped into the black and gold bass boat. A long, skinny man, his movements flowed like water.

"Lyle," Gun said.

Hedman stood on the floor of the boat, hands on hips. He wore a safari shirt and pants that were tailored to fit snugly around his tubular arms and legs. His fleshy, self-indulgent face belonged on a heavier body, and he kept it cocked to the left, showing Gun only the right side. "You going to shoot me?" he said. He was looking at the .38 Gun was holding.

Gun tossed it to him. "You're not an easy guy to drop in on."

From the prow of the boat came a low rumble. A huge Irish wolfhound sat there perfectly motionless, its face bearing an expression of intelligence and gravity. The dog's eyes were the same color as Hedman's, very light, the shade of watery beer.

Hedman laughed. "Don't mind Reuben, he's very obedient."

"I bet."

"And about the weapon"—Hedman held up the .38 delicately with two fingers—"believe it or not, we need them here." He spoke in an easy sibilant tone. "We've had trouble with vandals."

"Funny," said Gun. "I heard the same thing from Tig Larson a couple days ago and Carol Long this morning."

Hedman smiled thinly again. "A beautiful woman, Ms. Long. Stunning, wouldn't you say?"

"You noticed," Gun said.

"So . . ." Hedman brought his hands together. "What brings you out here? You're a man known for preferring his own company."

"A visit."

"Well, I'm going fishing. Come along?"

"You like to talk on the water?"

"Untie us," said Hedman.

Gun undid the lines and stepped into the boat. In five minutes they were anchored off the northwest shore of Hambone Island, out of the wind and a few yards from a stand of rushes. Hedman was casting out and reeling in smoothly, the rod like an extension of his thin arm. As he worked he got careless, and Gun saw why he was hiding the left side of his face. The flesh around the eye was proud and discolored beneath a heavy application of tan makeup powder. The eye itself didn't look so good either. A bloody red flag extended from the yellow iris all the way to the outer corner.

"Somebody hit you?" Gun asked.

Lyle's quick laugh wasn't convincing. "Hit myself. Had my truck up on the lift, changing the oil. The wrench slipped on the goddamn oil plug. Hurt like a bastard, I'll tell you."

"Always change your own oil?" Gun asked.

"Damn right!" Hedman flared. "Anything wrong with that?"

"Admirable," Gun said.

Lyle glared at him, then looked suddenly toward his line and set the hook mightily. The fish didn't put up much of a fight. It was a hammerhead pike and Lyle threw it back in.

"You know what I'm here about," Gun said as Hedman rebaited his hook.

"Why don't you just tell me and then I'll know for sure."

"My daughter seems to be missing, and I hear she was with your kid the other night."

Hedman's amorphous face didn't show a thing. His beer-colored eyes blinked a couple times. He took a deep breath. "Gun, I'm sure you remember the night you brought Geoff home, naked." He laughed and swung his line into the boat to remove a weed from the hook. "I was damn unhappy at the time, I don't mind telling you. But after I found out what had happened, what Geoff had done to those girls—after I cooled off a little—I realized that what you did to my kid was just what he needed." He cast his line again, then reached out and patted Reuben's large head.

"Mmm," said Gun.

"No, I mean it. You did the right thing, and I learned a lesson, a mighty hard lesson."

"Mmm."

"I learned it's pretty damned hard to recognize the fact that you've lost touch with your own kid."

"That's real nice, Lyle, but I came here to talk about Mazy, and I haven't lost touch with her."

"Just a minute now, hear me out. The fact is, last night Geoff and Mazy did go out together, and it wasn't the first time. Not by a long shot." He smiled, flashed his eyebrows. "Gun, our kids—"

"You and I both know that Mazy was on a story. Nothing more, nothing less."

Reuben made his presence known with a rumble, and Hedman stroked his neck.

"You're grievously mistaken, Gun." Hedman's eyes slid to starboard, where a Frisbee-sized turtle swam parallel to the boat, five or six feet away. He picked up a landing net from beneath his seat, eased it into the water behind the turtle, and thrust forward, snaring the turtle in the nylon netting. He dumped it upside down on the floor of the boat. Its underside was waxy and mottled in a geometric pattern of Halloween orange and sea green. Its legs clawed at the air.

Hedman looked up. "No, Gun. You're simply wrong about Mazy and my son. And as for Mazy's interest in Loon Country Attractions, I have nothing to hide. She was free to look at all my records, and I might add that her understanding of Loon Country's economic implications far exceeds yours."

"Well, that's good. Where the hell is she?"

"I don't know. And I don't know where Geoff is either. But I sure could guess who he's with. Look, last week my son told me things between him and Mazy were . . . heating up. He didn't come right out and announce anything, but I'm sure it was his way of sounding me out."

"Cut the crap."

The dog growled again, low muscular thunder rising up from its massive chest.

"You don't have to believe me."

"I don't believe you."

48

"Fine. But Geoff hasn't been home since yesterday. Haven't seen or heard a thing. My bet is that your daughter and my son have run off together." With his toe Hedman nudged the turtle, which had managed to right itself.

"If my daughter ran off with your kid," Gun said, "it's not because she wanted to. And if this thing has something to do with your development scam, you better believe I'm going to find out."

"I'll believe whatever I please," said Lyle, a little smile on his lips. "In fact, my inclination right now is to believe that you and I are relatives." He reached down and flipped the turtle upside down again. It tried to turn itself over with its head and legs, but Hedman took a toad stabber from his fishing box and sliced the turtle's craning neck from shell to mouth. Then he tossed the turtle into the water and it sank in a red cloud of its own blood. Reuben the dog whined, and bumped his nose nervously against the gunwale of the boat.

"Always hated turtles," Hedman said. "One bit me once, right here." He held up his right thumb for Gun to see a tiny white scar.

Gun said, "How about cats, you hate them too?"

Hedman looked at him quickly. "Depends on whose cat it *is.*" Behind the automatic smile, Lyle's face glistened with an emotion that looked for all the world like fear.

8

"All I can say is this, Gun. I've known your girl for a long time and I think I can read her pretty good. No way was she giving the nod to Geoff the other night. I don't care what the old man told you."

Gun nodded. After leaving Hedman's he'd driven straight over to Jack's and ordered lunch. It was eleven-fifteen.

"Lyle's full of shit, always has been," said Jack.

Gun finished his glass of buttermilk. Jack didn't know of the land transfer, and Gun wasn't about to say anything. Nothing he could say was going to make any difference now. If Mazy had married Geoff, then Lyle had the best land he could ever hope to ruin.

"You better tell me all the scuttlebutt you know about this Loon Country deal, Jack. Doesn't look like I can stay out of it any longer." He swallowed a bite of his burger.

Jack reached for the yellow carton sitting on the

shelf behind him. "What's Mazy told you? She'd know more than I would."

"Not much, as usual."

"Yeah." Jack refilled Gun's glass. "Well, it's hard to say right now. The referendum could go either way, is my guess. A lot of people support Larson, he's been a good commissioner for twenty years. On the other hand, you've got almost a majority of folks in this county getting their paychecks from Hedman, not to say they love the guy. His wife probably can't even do that. No, if you'd asked me two weeks ago, I'd have said Lyle's proposal wouldn't go through."

"But . . ." said Gun.

"But in the last dozen or so days Reverend Barr has really jumped on the bandwagon. He can make Hedman look like a prophet of God. And then there's that mock-up of Loon Country Attractions Hedman set up in the bank. Seen it?"

"No."

"It's impressive. The sort of thing that puts a picture in somebody's head. You don't forget it like you do a pretty speech. I'll tell you, though, looking at it, I couldn't help but wonder how the hell you're going to fit a condo, a world-class hotel, a shopping mall, a damn circus midway, and God knows what else—all of it on that scrap of swampland Hedman bought from Devitz. It doesn't add up."

"That's right, it doesn't."

"And don't forget the talking loon forty feet high. 'Greetings, friend. Welcome to Stony Lake, your entrance to the great northern wilderness.' Or some such shit. You feed it a quarter, it talks."

Gun stood up and reached for his wallet. Something was making his stomach uncomfortable, and it wasn't Jack's hamburger.

"It's on me," said Jack.

"Thanks." Gun rapped a good-bye on the bar, but Jack wasn't ready to let him go.

"What would Lyle want with Mazy, anyway? Say she did come up with something embarrassing—"

"Or illegal."

"Or illegal, right. Even if she did, Hedman isn't dumb enough to do anything to her. Damnit, Gun, what's going on?"

"Hedman seems to think he knows."

"You don't believe that rubbish any more than I do. None of this makes any sense." Jack picked up Gun's plate and glass and set them on the counter behind the bar.

Gun rubbed his jaw. He hadn't shaved yet today, and it was about time he did. Go home, shave, think, take a few swings.

"Well, does it?" Jack said.

Gun shook his head and took two steps toward the door. Then, on impulse, he turned. "You think maybe there's somebody bigger than Lyle? Somebody putting pressure on him?"

"What makes you say that?"

"You remember what I told you about Tig's cat."

"Sure."

"'Course we don't know Lyle was responsible, but say he was. Seems like a desperation move. There are better ways to go about persuading somebody."

"Filthy lucre," said Jack.

"And something else too. I think somebody knocked Lyle around a little bit, put the fear of God in him." He told Jack about Hedman's bruised face.

"That puts a little twist on things. Any idea who got the pleasure of smacking him?"

"Not yet," Gun said, "but let's give it some thought." He turned and headed for the door, stooping a little as he went. It opened as he reached for the knob, and Carol Long was there. She'd changed into khaki shorts and a Hawaiian shirt with a pink hibiscus pattern.

"Carol," Jack called from the bar. "You brought your legs. Good."

"Clever, Jack." Carol smiled at Gun. "He isn't well."

"Observant, though," Gun said.

"So am I." She tilted a look at him and glided over to the bar with a grace not often seen in Stony. She said, "Sorry I sprang in on you that way this morning. But I didn't understand things then, and I still don't. What about you?"

"I'm learning."

"Onerous process," said Jack.

"Well, I'm glad I found you. This morning I ran into Reverend Barr at Fisher's Café. Talkative man. You might be interested."

"Might be." Gun moved closer.

Carol Long crossed one leg over the other with a movement that was frank, even modest, yet the effect was no different than if the lights in the room had been snapped off to reveal she had glow-in-the-dark panty hose. But she wasn't wearing panty hose at all, and Gun had to take control of his eyes and tell himself to pay attention.

". . . and he was wearing his collar, dressed for preaching."

"It's eleven-thirty," Jack said. "He's probably in the middle of his sermon right now."

Carol shook back her hair like a schoolgirl. It was straight and black except for those rare gray strands that twisted off course like erratic pencil lines of light. She continued. "I'm sure he wasn't planning to come in—he'd already walked past the door. But when he saw me through the window, he turned around and came in, walked right up and asked if he could join me. I said fine."

She paused, looking first at Jack, then at Gun, before going on. "First off, he was acting smug, not unusual for him, I know. But he was the wrong kind of smug. There's the holy or intellectual kind that ministers and professors are great at, a benign loftiness. Barr's got that one down pat. But he was different this morning. This morning he was money smug. *In* the world and of it too. No platitudes or significant stares into infinity. Just plain physical arrogance."

"What did he say?" Gun asked.

"He asked if I thought my editorials against Loon Country were doing any good. I told him yes, I thought so, and he gave me this huge foolish grin. He was feeling so good he stopped a waitress and ordered himself breakfast." Carol lifted her chin and took a deep breath. Gun and Jack leaned in. "Then he looked around the café and whispered to me, 'I suppose you've heard the rumor about Hedman's new land deal.' I said no. He said, 'Well, it's no rumor. Lyle's got an iron-clad guarantee on the best property on Stony Lake.' Then he grinned again, real wide, and said he'd always wanted to leak a story to the press. And he left." Carol leaned back and was silent, bottom lip thrust out. She glanced from one man to the other.

Jack's face looked as solid as the mahogany bar that reflected its image. His dark eyes didn't blink. His forearms twitched in a kind of rolling motion from wrist to elbow. He said, "Everyone knows you've got the choice spot on this lake, Gun. What the hell's Barr talking about?"

Carol watched Gun's face.

Gun didn't answer, only sighed and withdrew behind a scowl that made his eyes disappear. From Jack's kitchen came the lazy sound of a country-western tune crackling through poor reception. Either Mazy had said nothing to Carol about the land transfer or else Carol was playing dumb. But the lines in her forehead looked earnest, and Gun figured she didn't know any more than what she was letting on.

"I think you'll be finding out soon enough," he said finally. He tipped his head slightly toward Carol Long and walked out of Jack Be Nimble's into aspen shade and brilliant splotches of noon sun.

9

The bells at Reverend Barr's church were doing their post-service chiming as Gun approached the edge of Stony. On impulse, he turned off Main Street and guided his truck along First Avenue toward the high-steepled edifice of red brick. He double-parked in front of it, sat with his elbow out the window, watching the parishioners file out the church doors and down the steps. Reverend Barr pumped hand after hand, often leaning close to offer words of either flattery or wit, judging from the response of his flock: nods or shakes of head, embarrassed shrugs, tossed hands—"Oh, you!" Gun wondered how Barr had managed to squeeze Loon Country into this week's sermon. According to Jack, a sometime church-goer, last week Barr had used the parable of the talents, that great New Testament defense of capitalism.

Now Samuel Barr was shaking County Commissioner Tig Larson's hand. Larson had a stiff smile on his face, an anxious set to his shoulders. He escaped quickly. As he turned onto the sidewalk, Gun eased the truck forward and pulled up alongside him.

"Hey, Larson. Surprised to see you're still attending."

Larson didn't slow his waddling gait.

"Larson!"

Larson turned, his face uncharacteristically wrinkled. He pointed at his watch. "Sorry, Gun, I'm kind of in a hurry. If you don't mind . . ."

"No problem." Gun accelerated, watching Larson in his rearview mirror. There was no use talking to him, anyway.

Turning back onto Main Street, Gun headed west. He had made a mistake signing his property over to Mazy. A bad mistake, no doubt about it. But it was done. The question now was how it happened. Had she transferred the land over to Hedman willingly or unwillingly? Had she been somehow forced into marrying Geoff—or was it her own free choice? Were they married at all?

Gun swerved to miss a squirrel dodging across the road, then down-shifted and turned north on the lake road, gave the big eight-cylinder some gas and shifted back up into fourth.

No, he simply couldn't feature it, couldn't even squeeze the two of them into his imagination at the same time. It was impossible. If his daughter was married to Lyle Hedman's son, it wasn't because she wanted to be. A chill shook Gun's shoulders and tingled clear out to his fingertips. He spoke out loud, in order to convince himself. "She wouldn't," he said.

The lake road was rough with potholes. The county men hadn't been around yet to repair the damage done by the recent winter's frost heaves. As Gun steered the Ford around Shipman's Bay he caught sight of old Leo Hardy, alone the last quarter century, standing tall and mackinawed on his dock. Leo waved, and Gun tapped two hoots on the horn. It was a little like looking at himself. Alone.

It hadn't been easy, giving Mazy up after the accident. It hadn't taken him long to see he'd done it all wrong, either. Her visits home were long and frequent, but her forgiveness was difficult to earn. They didn't fight—mostly since she didn't talk—but she went out of her way to show Gun he'd been wrong to let her go. Wrong to make her give him up when she needed a father most.

If it weren't for her dreams, Gun might have thought Mazy was just being stubborn, vindictive. But her dreams were real, and frequent. They arrived in the early hours of the morning, a week or so apart. She'd call out in a desperate voice, yanking him from sleep and setting him barefoot on the cold pine floor. He would walk into her room, turn on the light, and tell her everything was okay. She'd tell him what she'd just seen: the 737 tumbling out of control, its blinking red lights spiraling down through the night, the detonation of flame, the crack and whoosh of gas tanks bursting, the wavering pillars of orange terror shooting a hundred feet into the sky. And her father playing outfield under the bright lights at Bloomington.

Now, bumping along the rutted driveway, surrounded by the smells of weeds and flowers and pines, Gun asked himself if maybe his daughter resented him more than he knew. He parked the truck next to the garage. Stepping out onto the uncut grass, he heard the faint jingle of the phone ringing in his kitchen. He hurried only slightly, and picked it up in time to hear a click. He rolled a cigarette and sat at the table to smoke it. It would ring again.

It rang on his third cigarette. He picked it up.

"Hmm," he said.

"Dad?"

"Mazy." Gun sat down on the tabletop. "Mazy, are you all right?"

"I'm fine, great, just . . . really fine."

"Where are you? It's Sunday . . . I mean, we've been wondering where you are."

"With Geoff. Out at Hedman's. Got here this morning. In fact I just missed you, according to Lyle."

"What are you doing out there?" He had to ask, had to hear her say it.

"Dad?" The pitch of her voice was higher than usual. The tone harder. Her sentences shorter. "Dad, Geoff and I . . . we're married. We eloped, last night."

There it was. "You're in trouble, Mazy."

"No, really, I'm fine. You don't have to worry. I'll come and visit. Or no, why don't you come out here? Lyle says to tell you that you're always welcome. In fact, why don't you—"

"Tell me who it was that married you. Where'd you go?"

She said nothing.

"Tell me who married you and Geoff. I have to know."

"I don't know his name. A civil wedding, Ojibway County. The old guy that runs the hardware store in Blackstone. Something Gordon, I think."

"Sweetie, I'll do what I can. You know that. I'll do whatever I have to do." Gun was fingering the tobacco papers, but he didn't roll another cigarette.

"Come out, all right?" Mazy said. "Do that, okay? And about the land—"

"Forget the land, Mazy. Forget it."

"I've got to go. We'll talk later. We're about to have

dinner. Fresh walleye." She gave a little laugh that sounded almost cynical.

Gun was silent.

"Dad, I love you."

"You too," said Gun. "You know that."

"Yeah, I do. I've got to go now, okay?"

"Good-bye, Mazy. Don't worry now, all right?"

" 'Bye now."

"I said *all right?*"

She hung up.

He knew it wasn't any use but he made the call anyway. Zeke Gordon was pushing ninety, white cataracts on both eyes, the sort of man whose proximity to the next world puts soft colors on the present one. Every time Gun had seen him, the man was shedding happy tears about something. New kittens in the alley, bratty children playing in the street, the most recent couple he had joined together in holy matrimony back in the nail section of his hardware store on Saturday night.

Gordon sputtered through his gums, snapped his teeth into his mouth, and proceeded to carry on, congratulatory, weepy. Gun's pretty daughter had gotten married. Gun hung up on him.

A fresh box of baseballs had arrived yesterday from the store in Minneapolis, the first of a dozen sporting goods stores Gun had purchased after retiring. Gun went into his bedroom, fished out the box from under the bed, grabbed his bat from behind the bedroom door and went outside to load the pitching machine.

He couldn't remember being any better. His eyes were working so well he was able through concentration to make each pitch appear to slow down. He could see the red seams revolving, and merely had to put the meaty part of the bat on the ball. He took twenty swings and hit twelve baseballs out into the water, home runs. He lined seven into trees, and fouled off just one. The last pitch he sent deep to center field, and the ball hit a dead limb thick as a man's arm near the top of an old pine. The limb broke free at the trunk, toppled down and landed at the water's edge. The ball continued on.

10

The hearing next day was held in the upper-level dining hall of the Muskie Lounge, a plush green room used on occasions when the persuasion of comfort was needed. It held about 150 with all the folding chairs in use, and at a quarter to twelve the room was getting noisy with people talking at each other over complimentary drinks. A hush fell briefly as Gun walked in. Some turned and looked at him, but it wasn't long before the pitch of the room was back to normal.

Hedman was leaning against the wall at the front of the room, a prespeech drink in hand. Three smiling men in pastel suits stood around him talking. Above their heads was a mammoth wall-mounted muskellunge, a treble-hooked Rapala in its angry mouth.

"I bet he got that other land," said a woman's voice behind Gun. The voice was middle-aged with a cigarette scrape. Gun didn't turn around. "I bet he got it, and has this whole damn thing in his pocket."

"Got what other land?" said a male voice. "Who'd sell out to him? Besides, long as Larson's on the county board, this thing's just a dream." Gun smiled to himself. He hadn't been the last to find out after all.

"What do you think, that Larson's pure? Because he's a land and water freak? Or just because he's one of those nice honest faggots?"

"Aw, Melissa, you don't know that. And anyway, what if he is on the county board? It's going to a referendum. Popular vote, you know the concept."

"I'm serious," said Melissa. "Old man Hedman bought Larson just like he bought these drinks."

Gun turned his head just enough to suggest annoyance with the conversation.

"Shh," the man said.

Carol Long had arrived now and was moving gracefully among the county's overweight stratum of importance. Gun watched as she talked with Harold Amudson, her slender figure holding up a silver recorder the size of a cigarette pack. Harold Amudson was a town gas merchant. Until falling into Hedman's camp, Harold's idea of economic development had been to add another line of Little Debbie bars to the snack rack in his Standard station. Now he sold deli sandwiches and had a bright plastic roof over his gas pumps. Now he wore thin knit ties and bored anyone near him with schemes for development projects. There was a county board slot coming open in a year. Eight months before anyone cared, Harold was running for it.

"See you're waiting for me!"

Gun knew the voice. Geoff Hedman, tall and smiling, stood just within the wide double-entry. He wore a linen sport jacket, crisp Levi's, and a Key West tan. To his right, three ladies in bowling jackets ducked and whispered. "Looking fine," he told them. The women giggled.

Geoff walked through the center of the four lines of tables and straight to his father, who was still under the fish. Gun saw Hedman Senior speak to Hedman Junior and Junior nod a reply. Then Geoff stepped away from Hedman's group and walked toward the men's room.

Gun waited sixty seconds before following. Inside the men's room he could see Geoff's tan Armadillos tapping a worried waltz under the door of the stall. Gun looked in the mirror, squinted once to define the crow's feet, washed his hands, and leaned against a sink opposite Geoff's stall.

When Geoff swung open the stall door, Gun said, "I want to know one thing from you."

Geoff stood in front of the coughing toilet. "Mazy isn't here," he said. "She's at home, waiting for me."

"That wasn't the question." Gun shut the distance between them in two strides and stood in the john door, resting a heavy palm on each side. Geoff couldn't back up. "I want to know this. How did you force my daughter to marry you?"

Geoff's face looked straight ahead, eyes focusing on the line of Gun's T-shirt under his collar. "I didn't force her," he said. His lips spread into a satisfied smile. "We had to do it. We're in love."

Gun took his hands away from the metal stall and put one on each of Geoff's shoulders, gripping them as if to squeeze ball from socket. "I want you to listen," he said, and with a quick downthrust he buckled Geoff's legs and put his tailbone hard on the plastic toilet seat. He bent down to Geoff's face. "I want you to know that if my daughter is once touched in any way, if she is not treated as if your life depends on her safety, then I won't just sit you down on a toilet. I'll cram you inside one. And pull the chain."

Geoff didn't answer. Gun slapped the stall closed on his way out.

Every chair was filled when Gun stepped back into the meeting room. He stood against the rear wall, his flanneled arms crossed on his chest. The heavy noise of social anecdoting and backslapping had quieted now to a low wash of talk, jabbed by coughs and quiet laughs. The Reverend Samuel Barr was at the podium.

"Good friends," said Barr. "Good friends." His voice was low and powerful, traveling through the room at an almost subsonic level. People heard him, or sensed him, and ended conversations. "Good friends," Barr repeated, "I thank you all for coming today. The kind members of the county board have asked me to open this hearing, and I'd like to do so with a word of prayer." Barr bowed his head, displaying a bald circle at the crest of his scalp. Shanks of thick hair surrounded it in a gray halo. "Our Lord," he said, his voice humming like a bass guitar string, "we thank you for the opportunity of coming together today, and for the opportunity to speak out freely in a country made great by freedom."

In front of Gun a man in a red shirt gave his neighbor an elbow. "For the opportunity to drink top-grade scotch on a Monday noon," he whispered.

Samuel Barr continued. Gun saw a look of pious importance on the minister's narrow features. "We thank you also, Lord, for the chance to improve the lot you've given us. It's become easy for many of us who live here in this beauteous land of lakes and pines"— here Barr paused, as if thinking of specific names— "to forget that life is more than landscape. Life is the chance to work and earn, to give our children bread, to develop those resources we have at hand."

The prayer rumbled forth unhindered. Slowly the minister raised his bowed head, lifting his eyelids as if to spy on his somber audience. "We thank thee, Lord, for providing us with a means to a better life, that we might serve you more completely," he said. Barr and

Gun stood at opposite ends of the room, heads up, eyes wide, staring at each other over 150 sleepers. "We thank thee for allowing us this chance to restore our human dignity," Barr prayed.

"Dear God," Gun said quietly.

"And we ask that you would lead us now, help us to do what is right," Barr said. "Help us to help ourselves."

The man in the red shirt gave a single bronchial cough. Barr lowered his head and closed his eyes. "This is our earnest prayer, oh Lord, Amen."

"Amen," said several voices at the front tables.

"And now," said Barr, "I'd like to bring up Elder Hedman. People have been saying Elder's got a big surprise to spring. That true, Elder?"

Hedman uncoiled himself from his chair and moved jointlessly to the podium. Gun could see Geoff now, recovered from his rest-room trial, blushing near the door.

"Pastor," said Hedman, stooping as he reached the podium, "you have the *holiest* voice I've ever heard." A few people laughed. Gun rolled up slightly on his toes, leaning into the room toward Hedman. Geoff, to Gun's left, had his hands rammed deep in his pants pockets.

"It was a bigger surprise to me than it will be to you," said Hedman. "My boy Geoff ran out on me over the weekend and came back with a ring on his finger." Hedman unstooped his shoulders and stretched his thin lips in a grin. "The kid went out and eloped, and him a staid thirty years old." He shook his head as if in fond exasperation. "And the best part of it is, he went and found a woman you'll all agree comes from good, strong stock: Mazy Pedersen."

A hundred fifty faces turned to the back of the room. Hedman ran a slick tongue over his parted lips. Gun's eyes stayed on him. Hedman squinted and smiled narrowly, like a man spotting a bagful of money across a crowded hall. "Gun!" he said. "Gun Pedersen. *Damn!* Who'd ever thought we'd be relatives by marriage. Guess we never knew how bad our kids had it for each other."

"Guess not," Gun answered.

"Damn right!" Hedman said, celebratory. "And Gun, my friend, since our kids have gone and made everything a lot easier, maybe you'd like to announce the second part of the surprise."

"Floor's all yours," said Gun.

"Pleasure," said Hedman. "Ladies and gentlemen, I'm happy to tell you the way has been cleared to build Loon Country Attractions on a suitable site—not that eastside swamp. Provided the referendum goes through, and with the gracious permission of Geoff and Mazy Hedman, the biggest development in the northern half of the state will go up on the old Pedersen property west of town. Four hundred acres of prime lakefront. Room for the mall, room for hotel accommodations. Time-share condos. Theaters. Restaurants. Jobs. Loon Country Attractions will attract millions of customers a year." Hedman stopped. He ran his long fingers through his limp silver hair. He smiled with his upper teeth at Gun. "Mr. Pedersen," he said. "Why don't you come up and bless the marriage of our children."

Gun said nothing. He turned his head and caught Geoff looking at him. Geoff was immediately snagged with a fit of coughs.

"Later, then," said Hedman. "We'll have a private toast. In the meantime, this is a *public* hearing—a piece of democracy. Does anyone have something to say? Floor's open." Hedman stretched his long arms into a plea for someone else to talk. No one did, and he seemed about to give up and start another speech when Carol Long spoke.

"What about Larson? Let's hear what Larson thinks." Several voices affirmed the idea, and Hedman smiled at them.

"Of course," he said, and signaled Tig Larson to the podium. Larson was slow getting up and squeezed between the rows like a baby whale in a tight channel. He seemed to be breathing hard. "In the past, of course," Hedman said, "I've known Tig as an eloquent and worthy adversary. You all know his record as a conservationist. But now, fortunately for Stony, he's recognized that not all progress leads to Hell. Commissioner?"

Larson, large and moist in a light summer suit, gained the podium and rested there on his arms. Hedman stepped back and waited for him to speak. Gun saw Carol, sitting at a table on the room's left edge, printing precisely with a pen. Larson blew out his cheeks.

"I think there has to be a time when you look at certain realities," he said. "And I think this is such a time. I know it's important to keep our land and waters healthy. I know our lakes are under strain from farmland drainage and acid rain . . ." Gun tried to pin down Larson's eyes with his own, but Larson was watching his hands. "Still, we need the jobs. We need the tourism dollars. Mr. Hedman has promised me he'll guard against the destruction of the existing lakefront," Larson said. Hedman clasped his hands behind his back, nodding his acknowledgment. "I believe him," Larson said. "I'm asking you to vote yes on the Loon Country referendum."

Gun saw Carol's pen hand pause and her black eyebrows point up at the center. She turned to look at him, and he walked past Geoff out of the room.

11

At one o'clock a slow breeze from the east was reshaping what had been a pleasant forecast, and people were exiting the Muskie Lounge. Most seemed slightly dazed from Hedman's gift drinks, and willing enough to go to the polls with such generosities in mind. Gun stood in front of the lounge entrance. He was waiting for Larson.

He had to wait a long time. The first people out were mostly young, hurrying back to untenured positions, checking the creases in their slacks. Then came the sociable threes and fours, holding discussions about the pros of a paved tourist haven in the midst of pines and bright lakes. Gun didn't hear any suggestions about the cons. He stood at the T where the Muskie Lounge sidewalk met the grass boulevard and listened to the voices die when they passed him. A few said lopsided hellos, looking at Gun's chin when they spoke. He didn't answer. Hedman came out, taller and skinnier than most of his entourage. He was encircled by them, and they moved eagerly around him as if waiting for his autograph, never losing their places. Only Hedman seemed to see Gun as they went by, his beer-colored eyes glistening with confidence.

Larson came out near the end. His tie was hanging loose on his shoulders, and a shiny mauve undershirt showed at the neck.

"You've seen my land before," Gun said.

"Aw, damn," moaned Larson. "Now, suddenly, he cares."

"You've been over every foot of lakeshore. You've been there in the early spring, watching the walleyes spawn."

Larson closed his eyes. "Gun," he said. "I know."

"Explain."

"Can't do it," said Larson. He took a wasted step away from Gun and was halted by a hand against his chest. "Aw, Gun," he said, "it's not your land. It's not even Mazy's land now. It's Hedman's. Everything's Hedman's."

"Tell me something, Tig. How did Hedman know it was all in Mazy's name?"

Larson shrugged, looking down at Gun's hand, still hard against his chest. "How well do you know your lawyer?" he said.

"Not well enough, I guess."

Larson inhaled with effort, pulling air through a pinhole. "Gun," he said, "please let me go. I didn't know about his plan to get your land. Believe me, I would've told you. Now really, I have to go."

"It's not like you to back down, Tig. Hedman make good on those threats?"

Tig shrugged. "I didn't have any choice. Not this time, anyway."

"A person's always got a choice," Gun said.

Tig smiled, his eyes flaring. "Of course. And how about Devitz? That poor old bastard have a choice?

Did you know he died last night? Hear anybody at the meeting talking about that?"

Gun closed his eyes. "No. No, I didn't." He took his hand away. A sour knot rose in his stomach like yeast. Jeremy Devitz hadn't lasted a month without his land. "I'm sorry."

"I have to go," said Tig.

"Sure. Where to?"

"I don't know." His eyes closed, and when they opened they looked flat as the eyes of the dead. "Yes, I do. I'm going to Holliman's Bluff."

"It's a quiet spot," said Gun.

12

Nash Sidney's office, the only law office in Stony, occupied what had once been the town's only five-and-dime store until Ronnie Truman, the owner, had declared bankruptcy a couple years ago. Now Ronnie operated a car wash south of town and Nash Sidney spent a lot of time alone in his youthful practice on Main Street.

Or had spent time alone. It had been roughly a year since Gun visited him to formalize the transfer of land, house, and personal effects to Mazy's name, and Gun noticed a lot of changes in the formerly sparse office. For starters, when he pushed the door open, there was no dime-store tinkle.

"Hi, Gun," said Nash Sidney. He sat behind a big kidney-shaped desk new enough to smell like varnish. "Miss the bell?"

"You took it down," Gun said. "What would Ronnie say?"

Nash smiled. "He was here last week to talk about a

suit. Seems his car wash soaped and waxed the crushed velvet in some lady's Lincoln. Ruined it. She's suing Ronnie because she forgot to roll the window up."

"Glad you still care about client confidentiality."

"Anyhow, he never noticed the bell," Nash said. "I was disappointed." He rose, tall next to anyone but Gun, and leaned across the desk to shake hands.

Nash Sidney was twenty-eight years old, had graduated from high school a couple years ahead of Mazy and gone to the University of Minnesota on a sports scholarship. Baseball. His fastball and control had been the only happy factors on a sad Stony team for several years, good enough to draw scouts from at least two big-league organizations. Nash chose the university, which made Gun smile, and then law school, which made him sorrowful. Talent didn't belong in a toilet.

"Business good?" Gun said. He was looking at the kidney-shaped desk, which matched a set of gleaming walnut file cabinets on the back wall.

"Business is very good," Nash said agreeably. "I'm quite a happy lawyer. What summons you to town?"

"Big meeting today. Over at the Muskie. Surprised I didn't see you there."

"The Hedman event, yes. Um, congratulations." Nash sat down again and winced slightly, as though his chair was padded with rocks. "I'd have been there, but the phone wouldn't quit. I have one of those secretaries that only works mornings. You know."

"Yup." Gun sat down on the hood of Nash's desk. He inhaled through his nose and squinted at a blue-tinted map pinned to Nash's big bulletin board.

"Gun, what's going on?"

"I think I'm finding out. An onerous process, as Jack says." He nodded at the map. "Isn't that a blueprint for Hedman's mall project?"

"Loon Country Attractions. Yes."

Gun smiled. "You know, there's something familiar about that shoreline. The way it dips in right there, next to where you've got the talking loon. I wonder where I've seen that before."

Nash was quiet. He took off his glasses and dangled them in his fingers. "Good God. You mean you didn't know? Until today?"

"That Mazy was pulling out with Geoff? Or that my place, her place, is heading for the sewer? And how did you know about any of it, anyway?"

Nash shrugged. "I wouldn't call Loon Country a sewer. Mazy could do worse than Geoff Hedman. And I knew about it because I'm Lyle's lawyer. One of them, at least. He's been hinting about some such romance, and it wasn't hard to guess the rest. That map there," he poked a thumb at the wall, "is a prospectus. Something Lyle had drawn up, just in case it worked out."

"Just in case," Gun said. "I would have appreciated a call."

"Assumed you knew. You've got a daughter who has a little to do with this, Gun. Don't you and Mazy ever talk?"

Gun stood up. "Nash, I came in here a year ago and we made a legal transaction. Mazy knew about it and that was as far as it went. She didn't talk about it, I didn't talk about it. Not to anybody. Now I find out she's joined the Hedman household, and like it or not, she's serving up her inheritence so Lyle can build himself a kingdom on it. He knew about that land transfer somehow. Before he should have. And I wonder how."

Nash Sidney folded his hands. He looked at Gun as though sizing up a judge, put an appeal in his eyes and said, "I didn't tell him, Gun, if that's what you're thinking."

"That's exactly what I'm thinking."

"Gun, listen. Yes, I handle some private matters for Mr. Hedman. I'm his attorney, for God's sake. I've done some work on his Loon Country thing." Nash's tone now was backstabbed honesty. "But Gun, he gets no special favors in this office. And he hasn't asked for any."

Gun stood and rested his right hand on a swooping brass floor lamp that beamed down on Nash's desk. His eyes breezed through the room. "This has turned into a nice little practice for you, Nash. New desk, files, nice carpet. These errands you run for Hedman pay well."

"I have a lot of clients," Nash answered.

"And a whole bushel basket of new ones, once Loon Country is up and running."

Nash smiled involuntarily and squelched it. "Well, sure. It's a safe guess that new industry in town will bring along some legal holes to plug, and I'll be here to do it. That's my job."

"But that's all you'll get from Loon Country? A few more clients, maybe a full-time secretary? I'd think Hedman would be more grateful than that. Maybe make you his corporate legal advisor, give you a seat on the board." Gun sighed. Being nasty exhausted him, but he needed true words out of this boy.

"Gun, I'm not responsible—" Nash began, but Gun tightened his fingers on the floor lamp's neck and snapped his wrist upward. The brass knuckled back like a garden hose and the beam rested bright on Nash's face. Gun leaned down at the blinking lawyer.

"Tell the truth," he said, "and you'll get off easy. Think of it as a plea bargain."

Nash closed his eyes against the light and ran a long handful of fingers through his hair. Gun felt the confession working its way free. He waited.

Nash said, "Might've let it slip, I guess." He kept his

eyes closed, as if the words might look worse out in the light.

Gun straightened and walked to the door. Nash sat still under the brass lamp. Gun started to leave the office but was stopped by a thought and leaned back in.

"Nash. Why didn't you stick with baseball?"

The lawyer's eyes opened. They were watery as a child's. "I didn't have a curve, Gun. You remember."

"That's right." Gun shrugged. "Well, you've got a beauty now."

13

Gun drove out to the Devitz place after leaving Nash
Sidney's office, but Bowser wasn't home. Gun knew
where to find him.

Harrelson's Scrub was an unhappy 360-acre piece
of Ojibway County that had gone unlived on since the
early 1950s. That was when Margie Harrelson, as Gun
had heard it, had finally killed herself with the pure
mean hard work of farming land meant to remain
untilled. Margie left the land to the county when she
died. Her son didn't want it.

Gun slowed the old Ford and turned onto the
township gravel that ran along the south border of the
Scrub. Margie's house was as dead as she was, having
been taken back by rampant willows. Gun stopped the
truck and stepped out.

It was colder than it should have been. A gray north
wind blew moody clouds over the Scrub, clouds white
and the color of dead ashes. The willows and a few
malnourished oaks bent toward Gun in the wind, and

the brushy trees beneath them quivered. Gun's hair, white mixed with what was left of blond, flattened against his forehead. There was no open space on the Scrub that he could see, no sign that this land had ever been cleared for the plow, and there was no sign of Bowser. Gun reached back behind the seat of the Ford and pulled out a shirt of nappy brown wool.

Walking was difficult in the Scrub, but the wind was cut. Gun pushed his way through brush and grass that reached to his waist, and ducked his head from branch slaps. Down at his feet something that felt like barbed wire caught and ripped at his ankle. Gun reached down through thick growth and pulled up a reaching bramble. There was blood on the spines. Gun considered a swear word, then heard through the tangle of woods and weeds the sound of bursting glass.

"Bowser," Gun said, not too loud because the sound of glass had been very close.

"Present," said Bowser's voice. There was crunching in the brush and hard breathing, and then the Scrub parted and Bowser appeared. He was firm and fat, bearded and drunk. There was a mostly empty bottle in his left hand, bourbon, and a homemade slingshot in his right. "Happy day," he said.

"You're here." Gun sighed. His ankle smarted and he could feel his Pony runner absorbing blood. Bowser waved his bottle in invitation and Gun went with him through the thicket.

Bowser had set up a dark green ice-fishing shack near an old stock pond in the middle of the Scrub. The pond was brown, even in May. Bowser slapped the side of the fish house with the slingshot. "Built this lady in 'sixty-seven," he said. "With the old man. He by-God knew how to put things together." Bowser opened the plywood door and slammed it shut. "These many years and still as solid as earth. It's my goddamned home now and I'm glad of it."

"You still own the home place. Why aren't you there?"

"I don't own nothing." Bowser leaned back with the bottle and swallowed with his eyes shut. "The old man thought Hedman was doing him a favor, leaving us half an acre and the house. Shit."

Gun looked around at the Scrub. "Might be better than living out here."

"You don't believe that," said Bowser.

"I just heard about your dad," Gun said. "I'm sorry."

Bowser's eyes went to Gun's wounded ankle. "Hurt yourself," he said. He lifted the bottle toward Gun. "Medicine."

"Thanks." The bourbon was cheap and scraped a little on the way down, but the day was cool and Gun welcomed it. He sat down on an upturned five-gallon pail and looked at the ankle. The bramble had snagged him just above the shoe, drilled a neat hole in the flesh between the bone and forward tendon. The hole was deep and clean. He crossed the ankle over his good leg to keep it high, stop the bleeding.

Bowser had opened the fish house again and was sitting down in the narrow doorway. His big thighs were squeezed by the doorframe, and he leaned forward to give his shoulders room. Gun realized Bowser must have to enter the fish house sideways.

"Mr. Pedersen, say, have another and pass it on back."

Gun tilted another mouthful of bourbon. There was a splash of liquor still left in the bottle. Gun tossed it to Bowser.

"Ummm," said Bowser. He finished the bourbon and poked his little finger into the bottleneck. With strain he stood from the doorway and walked, the bottle swinging on his pinky, to a straight thin sapling not six feet tall. He slid the bottle neck down over the tip, and its weight bent the little tree south, with the wind. "For later," he said. Gun didn't understand, and didn't ask.

"So you're here out of kindness?" Bowser said it without sarcasm. "You're sorry about the old man, and maybe feeling bad after kicking my ass the other day?"

Gun smiled. Bowser had faults, but possessed the gift of truthful utterance. "Sorry about your dad, yes. Sorry he died without getting your land back from Lyle Hedman."

"People don't get things back from Lyle Hedman."

"Could be you'll be the first. You've heard about the change in plans? For the Loon Mall?"

"Sure." Bowser didn't seem interested. "He nailed my hind end, then he nailed yours. I felt bad, hearing about it."

"Well. Old Lyle's not going to need your place now."

"You're thinking I should take the money that skinny piece of dog shit gave my old man, go on over to the Hedman place and try and buy it all back."

"You could give it a shot." Gun reached for the Pony runner he'd taken off. "Worst thing Hedman can do is say no. Or jack up the price."

Bowser put his chin down into his neck and snorted, raking his throat for phlegm. He found some and sent it out into the Scrub. Then he turned and went around the corner of the fish house.

When he came back he was carrying a green Coleman cooler. It matched the paint on the fish house. Bowser opened the cooler and brought up a sealed bottle of bourbon. He peered through it at the sky for an instant before twisting off the cap and sampling.

"You know, Mr. Pedersen," Bowser said, "I don't think I want that land back."

Gun finished tying on the Pony runner. He stood up. The ankle was stiff but held him upright.

"I think Hedman can keep it and use it or not use it, may he land with a bump in Hell," Bowser said. He put the bottle down in the grass and withdrew the slingshot from his back pocket.

Gun waited. The swallows of bourbon were gone from his blood and the wind was stiff and chill.

"Because," Bowser said, searching at his feet for a stone and finding one, "if that bastard puts up his goddamn mall, on your land or mine, no matter, you're not going to see my great white butt anywhere within fifty miles of it. I'll go north, or I'll go west like my old man. But you won't see me here." Bowser had the stone fitted now and pointed the slingshot almost without looking. He pointed it at the bottle hanging at the tip of the swaying sapling. He pulled the stone almost all the way back to where the black whiskers began on his cheek, and then he let it go. It flew with bulletlike trajectory, passed through the waistcoat of the dapper gentleman on the bourbon label and dropped pieces of bottle into the grass. The sapling sprang upward, pointing to heaven.

Bowser tossed the slingshot onto the cooler and looked at Gun.

"The bare-naked truth," he said.

14

The drive home was cool and whippy with the windows down. Gun could see a mountain range of sea-colored clouds in the rearview mirror of the old F-150. The clouds were diagonally split by a silver shaft where the mirror was cracked. During the hunting season of '73, when the truck was only two years old, Gun's 30–06 Springfield had rocked out of its back-window saddle on a bad pothole. It bounced forth unloaded, gave Gun a brief crack on the skull, and spun its smooth trigger guard into the mirror. Gun hadn't fixed it since then, and had never again put a firearm into the rack. Now he slid them under the seat.

A mile west of Stony on old County 70 Gun shifted down and turned right on the lake road. He followed it through trees that leaned in to cover the sky: tall black-bruised birches, second generation pines from cones tromped on by waves of loggers, slender aspens brush-stroking in the light wind. Little rips and tears of sky between leaves were blue and getting bluer, the color swelling with humidity the way Minnesota afternoons do before a night rain. Gun slowed the truck and smelled the air like a hound.

Home was left off the township road and three quarters of a mile down a double-rutted truck trail. Weeds exploded from between the ruts, giving the trail a wild look that Gun liked. Cars full of cotton-print tourists didn't drive in to ask directions.

He had left the right rear burner of the gas stove on. The kitchen was warm and smelled like a winter evening, and mixed with the rising humidity, it was uncomfortable. Gun put out the flame and slid up all the windows that weren't already open. Then he went to the bedroom to change.

When he reentered the kitchen to make lunch, he was wearing cutoff Levi's white from use and a blue short-sleeve work shirt with the armpits ripped. A year ago Mazy had raided her father's dresser and used the shirt to wax her 1968 MG. Gun, in turn, had raided the trash at six o'clock on a Tuesday morning to recover it before Gurney plowed in with his garbage truck. There were still bruises of pink paint dust on the shirt. Gun had saved it for its ripped armpits. They allowed him to swing a bat freely, or a shovel.

There was little food. Gun opened the dank cabinet under the sink and found some potatoes sending colorless shoots through the holes in the plastic sack. There was Dinty Moore beef stew in the cupboard, and several cans of ravioli. Gun opened the refrigerator and saw a lump of dark cheese in Saran Wrap, a carton of eggs, half a gallon of yellow buttermilk. He sat on the kitchen table in his shorts, holding the refrigerator open with an extended Pony runner.

He tapped the fridge door closed and lifted himself off the table, the backs of his legs sticking to the varnish. The air was thickening. He went to the door and stepped out, bending to feel the untrimmed foxtails that angled out from the foundation. They slipped squealing through his fingers. He ripped out a handful and tossed them up, and they drifted down in the direction of North Dakota. Rain tonight. Gun went back to the refrigerator and took out the carton of buttermilk and the eggs. He also broke from the freezer a block of ice cubes which he dropped with much snapping and splitting into a gallon jar of tea the color of sunsets. He put the tea by the door. Then he poured most of the buttermilk into a multi-buttoned Hamilton Beach blender, cracked in four of the eggs, and frothed it all using the button farthest to the right. He took the pitcher off the blender, retrieved the ice tea, and carried both out of the house and down the hill.

Gun's stone boathouse was a project only a few days old. It would be a replacement for an earlier one, a husky slabwood structure he had built to defend his open Alumacraft from storms and Stony Lake breakers. Its performance had been perfect for a decade until this spring. A tight nor'easter had marshaled itself high over innocent farms in Ontario, taken a dip down and to the left over International Falls, and then, gaining speed, had suddenly dropped out of a dark cloud and come riding over Stony Lake like a chariot, blowing the tops of the waves into grapeshot spray. With his back to the heat of an April fireplace, Gun had stood at the window and watched. It took the wind and waves three minutes to put the boathouse asunder, and when the air was free of slabwood, he had gone out and yanked the dented Alumacraft up into the outfield grass.

Now there was nothing on the lakefront but a clean square hole. Gun had sandbagged a small dry area where the hole opened out onto the shore, and had spaded out and poured eighteen-inch footings. The old boathouse hadn't had the benefit of a solid anchor. This time he would build on rock. Not for himself— he wasn't going to be here. Probably not for anybody. But it made him feel useful, defiant. And it was a good habit: finish what you start.

A hump of spray-cleaned lake stones lay on the grass next to the hole, stones that Gun had weeded from a walleye bed not a quarter mile out. Gun figured there were enough rocks for four feet of solid wall on three sides before he'd run out. Again he sniffed the air for wetness.

He went to the small shed, where bits of scrap slabwood waited for the chainsaw, and came back with a hundred pounds of cement dust in a bag over his shoulder. In his other hand was a large steel bucket containing a triangular trowel. He ripped open the string-stitched bag and poured about half the dust into a fifty-five-gallon drum between the footings, then added buckets of water from the lake and stirred and slapped at the gray mud until it was flabby and made noise like the quicksand in old Tarzan movies. As he moved the trowel over the footings, laying a base for the bottom tier of stones, Gun felt the first stiffening of the small east breeze.

She's at home, waiting for me. It made Gun's mouth sour to think of Geoff's soft hands on her. Couldn't be true. Was not true. He picked up one of the stones from the pile, hefted it to his shoulder, guessed its weight at twenty-five or thirty pounds, took three quick steps toward the water and heaved. The rock came down, *thump,* twenty yards out.

He had put down four layers of rock and forgotten his buttermilk and tea. He stood straight up between the growing walls, stripped away the soaked shirt and saw the pitcher and jar sweating to match his own skin. Careful not to disturb the newly bedded lakestone, he vaulted out of the hole and dispatched more than half the buttermilk and egg mixture. It cooled and slightly sickened him, and he could feel his shoulder and neck muscles rock. He traded the pitcher for the gallon of tea, watery now. The cold jar balanced with a wholesome weight in Gun's wide palm as he tilted it up. The sky was sinking down for an early night. Half the pile of rocks was still on the ground.

Back in the hole, Gun troweled thick mud between rocks and packed more rocks on top and beside, eyeing from the pile just the right stone to fit each circumstance. Mazy had helped him build the first boathouse when she was fifteen, reluctantly handing him nails to put between his teeth. Today she had not even been at the meeting where it was announced that her land would soon be dead and interred beneath cement and glass and tourists.

The rock pile disappeared a quarter of an hour before the cloudburst. It was enough time for Gun to take a mouthful of warm egg buttermilk, spit it away, swim once out to the walleye bed to rinse away the grit, and go inside to bed.

15

Tuesday came up light blue and warm, the blurring humidity washed out of the sky by what Gun estimated had been a two-inch downpour. The rain had muddied the walls and floor of Gun's boathouse hole, but hadn't damaged the mortar work. The gray cement had set up fast, and now held trails of silt and dirt between the rocks where the water had run. No more masonry for the present.

The grass and weeds soaked Gun's tennis shoes as he walked to the infield. He kept the bat on his shoulder. He wanted it dry for contact. The pitching machine, tarped against the rain, had come through the storm honorably. With his free hand Gun undid the twine holding the tarp and pulled it into a heap behind the mound.

The machine undraped, wheels spinning, tripod legs quivering, a dozen baseballs counting down to blast-off, Gun waited patiently at home. On mornings this light he sometimes smote baseballs so far his eyes lost them in the general whiteness of the sky. More than thirty years ago he'd done the same thing in front of a major-league scout, who told him that frequent repetitions would earn him a substantial and enjoyable living. It turned out that way.

Now the machine ticked and trembled, and a ball was seized and spun toward home at big-league velocity. Gun swung and made slight contact, launching the ball nearly straight up. He counted a hang time of eight before the ball came down just back of the machine. The arm snapped again, and this time Gun sent a hard grass burner through the hole between third and short. It sent up a thin cloud of spray that rainbowed briefly in the sunshine. Gun shook his head and twisted the bat in his hands. He jabbed his toe at the ground. Inhaled, kept his lungs full. The next pitch came in chest high, and the club end of the Hillerich and Bradsby met it hard, a fraction of an inch below center. The ball rose outward, lakebound. He tried to follow its course but the white morning air had sunspots. It was lost until the distant *hock* of belted water.

"I saw Jim Rice do that at Fenway once," said Carol Long. She was standing in the weeds behind Gun and to the left. In the third-base dugout.

"Sweet heaven," Gun said. "You're early. Game doesn't start till one."

"I always come for batting practice." Carol stepped out of the tall grass and into some that showed her ankles. She wore green spring walking shorts. "Go ahead," she said. "Hit a few more."

"I'll hit later," said Gun. The machine clicked and fired, and Gun held out the bat in an impromptu one-hand bunt. "Had to stop it," he explained. "Sometimes they get lost in the grass."

"Or the lake," said Carol.

Gun walked to the pitching machine and killed it

just before it kicked into another fling cycle. He turned to Carol, who was standing now in the region of the coach's box. Her arms were crossed. Gun smiled. One season crossed arms had been a signal to steal. The next year it meant look out for the pickoff. "I'm glad to see you," he said. "Should I be?"

She waved a legal-sized notebook. "I'm working on a story . . ."

"Ah, you journalists."

Carol uncrossed her arms now and started toward him. "You know, I've lived in Stony nearly a month now and never seen the much-bespoken Gun Pedersen land," she said. "Or not much of it."

"You want to find out exactly what it is Hedman's trying to trash."

Carol had reached him at the pitching machine. There were a few thin leaves of pale wet grass sticking to her ankles, just above the sandals.

"I didn't know about it myself until the day before yesterday," Gun said. "Or know for sure."

Carol's green shorts had abstract white designs. On top she wore a loose white cotton pullover with wrinkles at the shoulders.

"I've decided not to let them do it," said Gun. It was a statement that he hadn't known was true until he spoke.

Carol's face was direct and proportionate. No needless flesh on chin or cheek. The fall of her bangs across her forehead stirred in the breeze. Her perfume was something of island origin, and near enough to feel.

"Would you like me to show you around?" said Gun. He made an exaggerated gesture with his hand. "Yes."

The four hundred acres made for a long morning's walk. Gun showed Carol the coastal hollows that changed shape with each spring's gouging ice-melt, a sudden twenty-acre clearing where the trees fell off to willowy shrubs and then to rushes, the clear-running stream that left Stony Lake and headed west. Finally they climbed a small rise at Gun's northern boundary. Underfoot was a cushion of needles and above rose some of the last virgin pines in the logbelt.

"They were here," Gun said, staring up, "before anything."

"Like the redwoods in California." Carol tilted her head back. "What kept the loggers from cutting them down?" she asked.

Gun kept his eyes on the treetops. "I guess when the first loggers got here there were still some Indian legends around. One of them was about a young Chippewa chief named Mountain Face, who was a giant. Taller than four canoes are long."

"Large fellow," said Carol.

"Yup. And this Mountain Face died during a hard cold winter by going without food so the tribe could eat. They buried him up here."

"So the loggers stayed away? I'm surprised."

Gun winked. "The legend goes on to say that when Mountain Face's burial ground is violated, he'll come alive again, madder than hell. Maybe the loggers didn't want to chance it."

Carol said, "I thought the loggers had Paul Bunyan on their side."

"It's only a guess, but I think Paul Bunyan would have walked on tiptoe to keep from bothering Mountain Face."

"And Lyle Hedman?" said Carol.

Gun turned to look at her. The sun was touching her black bangs, highlighting the few silver strands. A trace of perspiration sparkled on her cheekbones. "What do you think?" he said.

Carol waited to answer until Gun shrugged and took the first step back toward home. Then she said,

"I think Lyle Hedman should step carefully. Old legends have a way of coming back."

"All right, journalist, what have you got?" Gun said. They were sitting on Gun's log porch holding stoneware mugs of ice tea.

Carol frowned and leaned back in the rough-hewn chair. "I'm having a hard time finding the handle, if you want to know the truth, Gun," she said. "I think it's about time you leveled with me, told me what your gut says." Carol took a sip of tea without removing her eyes from Gun's face. "Did she want to marry the guy or not?"

Gun laughed and looked away. "I've been trying not to think about it. Doesn't do me a bit of good. The more I think, the more I don't know, and the muddier everything gets." He tapped a finger against his head. "I can tell you one thing, though. If I knew she was in some kind of trouble I wouldn't be sitting here like this. But at this point what can I do? Roar in and sweep her away?" Gun stabbed a finger into the palm of his hand. "I've got to find a reason, one good reason. Something that'll tell me she needs help. I don't have that yet."

Carol nodded.

Gun leaned toward her. "How about you? What do you think? You're a friend of hers—she probably talks to you more than she does me."

"I don't know. She mentioned Geoff a few times. Told me about that night in the woods, the prank he and his friends pulled. She said how much she hated him."

"Bastard."

"But she also said—about a week ago, after she'd started the story—how she was beginning to understand him. How the two of them had things in common. Powerful fathers, the fear of not living up to expectations, you know. She said she was almost getting fond of Geoff, much as she hated to admit it."

Gun snorted and waved off her words.

"No, I'm not blowing it out of proportion. I'm just telling you what she said. Myself, if I had to guess, I'd say . . . oh, I don't know." She threw up her arms and sighed.

"You'd say what?"

"I just don't know."

"So we have to wait and keep sniffing around," Gun said, disgusted. "I wasn't made for this."

"Say." Carol brightened. "There was something Mazy mentioned, something I meant to tell you. She told me about it before I left for Minneapolis last week. She didn't know if it was important, but it had her stumped."

Gun waited.

"Loon Country's a four-hundred-million-dollar project, right?" said Carol. "And supposedly all the money's lined up: the local efforts are on track and coming together pretty good, considering the fact that nothing's official yet. Bond sales, pull tabs, stuff like that. And the heavy hitters are committed. Tynex in Minneapolis for a hundred mil, Diamond Inns, all of those you've heard about. But here's the thing. Mazy said she was looking through the portfolio at Hedman's projections and it all added up to about three hundred million, a hundred short. She showed her figuring to Lyle and he just laughed and pointed to a name on the list of investors. 'The balance is right here,' he told her."

"Who was it?" said Gun.

"I don't remember. I'd never heard it before."

"You don't remember anything?"

"I don't know, but I want to say it sounded African. It was a foreign word, I think. Yes, I'm sure it was."

Gun spent the next five minutes trying to jog Carol's memory, but nothing clicked. Then she looked at her watch and said she needed to get going, there were interviews to do before press time. "Wait a minute, though," she said, frowning suddenly. "Tig Larson."

"What?"

"I didn't tell you. But apparently he never went home after the hearing yesterday."

"Probably headed for Minneapolis," said Gun. "He has friends there."

"I don't know. There was a county board meeting last night. Larson doesn't usually miss those—and he wasn't there. And Chief Bunn was looking for him this morning. Stopped by the paper to see if I'd seen him."

"Bunn? What did Larson do?"

"Nothing. I guess Larson's garage was empty and the door was open and the storm last night rolled the neighbor's trash can in next to the Lawn Boy. It spilled all over. Bunn just thought it was strange that Larson wouldn't be there, cleaning stuff up."

Gun frowned and rubbed his forehead with the sweating mug. It made a vertical pink mark on the skin.

"I saw you talking to him after the meeting," Carol said. "What did he seem like?"

"He seemed like a tired, frustrated, out-of-shape environmentalist. He was depressed and a little drunk. And scared, maybe."

"He didn't mention if he was leaving town?"

"Nope. He said something about Holliman's Bluff, like he might do some fishing."

"Fishing?" Carol looked off toward the water. "Maybe he thought he owed it to himself after that performance at the lodge." She lifted the stoneware mug but stopped before touching it to her lips. Gun was on his feet and his face was gray.

"What kind of car are you driving?" he said.

"A Horizon," Carol said, "but I don't like it."

"We'll take the truck," said Gun.

They were quiet on the ride, partly because the old half-ton Ford made a lot of noise at seventy-five miles an hour. Holliman's Bluff was thirteen miles away, a dramatic chunk of upthrust rock that rose square-chested from the lake to a height of forty feet. There was a sign at the crest where the highway bent away from the lake: HOLLIMAN'S BLUFF—SCENIC PARKING. There was room for half a dozen cars. On summer nights boys in family rods brought their girls to the bluff for especially scenic parking, while below them men in silver and red Lund boats fished for walleyes on the shelf. The sheer rock cliff went straight down about ten feet into the water, then stuck out its shelf like a knee for several yards and dove again to lake bottom and a final depth of a hundred feet in years with lots of rain.

No one was parked at the bluff now, and no boats were working the shelf. Gun and Carol walked to the edge and looked over.

"What exactly are we doing here?" said Carol.

"I hope to God we're wasting our time," said Gun. He shaded his eyes with the flat of his hands, squinting down into the water.

"What do you see?" said Carol.

"Nothing."

"What are you looking for?"

"A county commissioner."

"Yes," said Carol. "God."

Gun glared at the water for another two minutes. Then he walked back to the truck and stood eyeing the parking area in front of the bluff.

"You're looking for car tracks," said Carol.

"The rain wrecked any that might have been here. I think I can see where a set of tires bent down the grass right there, near the edge, but I can't be sure. Maybe I'm inventing it."

Carol said she couldn't see the tracks. Gun said, "I think we'd better check." Kneeling, he untied and slipped off the Pony runners. He pulled off the loose T-shirt he was wearing, walked barefoot to the edge of the bluff, hiked his eyebrows twice at Carol, and dove.

16

Stony Lake in May was clear and arctic. The depth of the lake kept it colder than most, and the algae were not yet in bloom. Two months ago a car driven over Holliman's Bluff would have crashed and burned on thirty inches of pack ice. Now Gun's eyes stung with cold as he opened them underwater, searching.

He found nothing on his first dive. The spring runoff had been high this year, and the pull down to the shelf felt farther than ten feet. He maintained a depth of about six, his head humming from the pressure, and kicked slowly, following the shelf off to the left. He surfaced, blowing, thirty yards farther along the bluff from where Carol stood.

"Anything?" yelled Carol. She bent forward over the edge, the wind pushing her bangs aside and kiting the cotton shirt.

Gun shook his head, panting to replace the air he'd spent underwater. He floated easily, waving his numb limbs while the oxygen penetrated. When he felt strong enough he went down again.

He found Larson in his gray Buick Century another twenty yards along. The Buick was parked on the shelf with the right wheels hanging off the edge so it tilted like a car driven up on a curb. Larson was floating in the confines of a seat belt and shoulder strap, only lightly touching the seat. His heavy face was looking straight up through the custom-installed sunroof of the Buick, toward sunlight and air ten feet above. The mauve T-shirt stretched and rippled at the neckline. Gun pushed away from the car and let himself rise to the surface.

"He's here," Gun called to Carol. She had followed his course along the top of the bluff, and because of the slope, was now above him just twenty or so feet away.

"God, oh," said Carol. Her hands were clamped into fists, thumbs enclosed. She jammed them in the pockets of her shorts.

"I think I'd better bring him up." Gun shook his head to throw the water from his eyes, pulled in a heavy lungful of air and bobbed under.

He reached the Buick again and opened the door. It swung in slow motion, and he reached in and unclipped the seat belt. Larson was stiff in his sitting position, and his knees whacked against the steering wheel when Gun snagged his collar and tried pulling him out. The Buick rocked softly on the edge of the shelf, and he realized the need for care. If the car went over the side carrying Larson, it would take equipment and divers to bring Larson up. Not that it mattered too much. But Gun eased his approach a little. With the blood bumping in his arteries, already almost airless, he reached forward and straightened Larson's legs at the knees.

The commissioner's hands floated an inch above his lap, and Gun saw and barely registered that several of his fingers were missing, cleanly nipped at the second joints, thin petals of skin swaying out from the stubs. Stony Lake had an eager population of turtles. Gun clenched the muscles in his jaw and closed his eyes. *Air.* He opened his eyes, put a hand out to take Larson by the waving hair, and leaned him out the door. He pulled hard. When the legs cleared the wheel he yanked Larson clear, gripped a solid thigh and shoved the body skyward. Larson drifted up through twilight, legs straight out in front, face turned up. He looked like a child sitting on the floor, staring at a spider on the ceiling. He spun slowly as he rose. *Air.* Gun pushed off from the shelf and broke the surface in seconds, beating Larson to the top.

"Can't you get him up?" Carol said, almost before Gun's head pushed up into the waves. A ruffling breeze was coming from the northwest.

Gun was too busy refilling to talk. He motioned with his head at a spot a few feet to his left. Larson was unhurriedly surfacing there.

"Oh no," said Carol.

"I'm going to look through his car," said Gun, breathing hard. "Then I'll tow him in."

"I'll take your truck," Carol said, "get the police. God, does he have to *look* that way?"

"Wait," Gun said. He shook white slaps of hair off his forehead and blew hard through his nose. "Wait till I get ashore. For the cops." Then he was down again.

The glove box of the Buick held a Rand McNally map of Minnesota with a detail of Minneapolis and St. Paul on the reverse side. It held two empty bottles of Extra Strength Tylenol. A thin black jackknife with a fold-out fingernail file. Nothing else. Gun's lungs were fatiguing more quickly after several dives. He sent a hand rifling under the front seat, found nothing, then took the keys from the ignition and worked his way back to the trunk. There was a rubber doughnut and a jack, neatly screwed into place in the floor of the trunk. An empty yellow Heet bottle floated up and out past Gun's face. He felt heavy and sleepy in the brain. Not bothering to close the trunk, he dropped the keys over the edge of the shelf, bent over and grasped the rear wheelwell, and heaved the Buick into a slow fall. He didn't stay to watch. There was no percussive *thumm* through the water when it hit bottom. Gun came up next to Larson.

"What took you so long?" Carol sounded angry. Her clenched hands were paper-white. "You were down there forever."

Gun shook his head, swam a tired stroke to Larson and set off for a shallow slope of shore with the county commissioner riding behind.

The Stony authorities had not been confronted with a body for over two years, not since the last time Funny Harbon Starling and his buddy Jerry had gone sprinting over thin ice in Harbon's Power Wagon. It was something the two of them had done every November for fourteen years, proving their manhood. Finally the ice opened and swallowed them, burping up the bodies in the spring stormwash. Sheriff Bakke had turned white at the scene and threatened to turn in his badge.

Bakke was at the bluff now along with two cops, and blinking rapidly at Larson. "When was the victim last seen alive?" he said. The blinks were magnified by massive lenses in brown plastic frames.

Come on, thought Gun, find the right script. "I saw him yesterday. At the public meeting. Most of the town did."

"When did you locate the victim?" said Bakke, scribbling with the steno pad close to his face.

"Thirty, forty minutes ago."

"Thirty or forty minutes? Lord, Pedersen, why didn't you call right away?"

"I didn't think you'd be able to help him," said Gun. Carol, at his side, was rubbing him down with his shirt.

Bakke sighed. "The victim was in his car?" he said.

"Tig was in his car," said Gun.

"In a seat belt, you said."

"One of those habits it's hard to break."

"Car's still down there?" said Bakke.

"It was too heavy for me," said Gun. Carol smiled.

"We'll call you," said Bakke. He turned and walked to the two policemen, who were gesturing over the body. "I don't know," he said to them. "I don't know about this job sometimes. Law enforcement. *Shit.*"

"I need to get dry," Gun said to Carol. The northwest wind was steady and the waves were getting higher and farther apart.

"Your keys," said Carol, holding them out between thumb and pinky.

"You drive."

At home Gun put on dry blue jeans, and sweat socks under the running shoes, and a long green chamois shirt to restore the body heat lost in the lake. Carol poked through a *Baseball Abstract* on the kitchen table.

"Do you need to get back to the paper?" Gun asked her, returning to the kitchen.

"Deadline's eleven o'clock tonight," Carol said. She smiled. "I'd better get back by ten."

"Let's take a drive, then."

"Where to?" Carol leaned over the table at him, her hair falling ahead at the sides.

Gun held up a small triangular wad of paper. It was wet and clumped together, but the words printed on it were legible. He tossed it on the table.

"The Back Entrance." Carol looked up. "A bar napkin? I never heard of the Back Entrance."

"You will if you stay in Stony long enough. I found it on Larson when you drove up to Podolske's to call the cops."

"God. You searched the body. Shouldn't you have given them the napkin?"

"Given it to Bakke?" Gun shrugged. "He wouldn't have done anything with it."

"What's there to do? It's a bar napkin. What good does it do you?"

Gun shrugged again. "Don't know. Are we going for a drive?"

"Will we talk on the way?"

"If you like."

"Let's take my car then," said Carol.

When they were in the car, both of Carol's hands at the bottom of the plastic steering wheel, she said, "What's with the Back Entrance?" The front seat of the Horizon was pushed back to its outer limit. Gun's knees were against the dash. The Back Entrance was thirty miles to the south.

"It has a reputation," Gun said, "for being the kind of place people such as Larson like to go."

"Larson the homosexual, not Larson the environmentalist."

"Right."

Three miles later Carol said, "Why are we following Larson's backtrail?"

"I can only think of one reason right now," said Gun. "Mazy."

"I'm missing a link somewhere."

"Hedman. What if he knew what everyone suspected—that Larson was gay—and could prove it? What if he threatened to, um, expose him?"

Carol made a so-what sound with her lips. "Gun, that's ridiculous. A gay going public isn't a big deal."

"Hold it," Gun said. "You've got to remember, Larson was first elected commissioner twenty years ago. Just a kid out of grad school. Folks were proud of him, you know, Stony's clean young man. He had one of those green ecology stickers on the back of his Beetle. Real activist. Caught the guy from the old Shell station dumping used oil in the Woman River. It made Tig almost a folk hero for a while. And in Stony, folk heroes don't come gay."

"But everyone seemed to know Larson was gay anyway."

"Look," said Gun, "in a small town it's one thing for everyone to think they know some dirty little secret. It's another altogether when the secret is made public."

"Okay, if I give you that point, can you show me a connection to Mazy?"

"Hedman might be a swindler and a blackmailer," Gun said, "and maybe much worse. And he has Mazy. I think that's connection enough."

Carol was silent. Gun said, "I should just go in. Go in and get her out."

"You haven't given her a chance," said Carol. "She hasn't asked for help."

"Has she been able to?" Gun shifted his knees and the red plastic dash bent and creaked.

The Horizon, engine racing at fifty miles an hour, passed a garish homemade sign featuring a man with hairy legs and a raincoat. THE BACK ENTRANCE, it said. SEVEN MILES AND TO YOUR RIGHT. SEE YOU THERE.

"This is turning out to be not so much fun," said Carol.

"I know. And *you* can move your legs."

17

The Back Entrance had the tucked-under look of a basement house or a 1950s bomb shelter. It sat squarely next to the county blacktop, with a short gravel driveway and a ten-car parking lot. A sign on the door said BACK ENTRANCE LOUNGE.

"Do you see any guys in raincoats?" said Carol.

"Nope." Gun took his deepest breath since his swim near Holliman's Bluff and got out of the Horizon. He could feel a rubbing in his kneecaps as he stood up straight.

"I think we got here too soon," said Carol. "No one's here."

Gun walked slowly to the edge of the parking lot and peeked around the building. He saw a banged-up brown dumpster under a cloud of flies, and behind it an early seventies yellow Toyota Corolla. "It's business hours," he called to Carol. "Let's go in. I'm dry as Ezekiel's bones."

Eyebrows high, Carol pushed at the door. It swung

open. The place seemed larger on the inside, with the low-hanging lamps turned down to a glow.

"It's an optical illusion," said Gun. "You walk into a dark cave and it seems huge until somebody flicks on a light, and then it's as big as your bathroom."

"Are you sure there's someone here?" Carol spoke in a whisper.

"Should be," said Gun. His voice was at normal volume but seemed big in the dark. "There's a car out back. The door was open." He walked ahead of her, easily skirting the barely-lit chairs and tables.

"Ouch," said Carol. "Shinned a chair. How can you see in here?"

"Pretty well," said Gun, then turned up his voice. "Hey, Toyota," he called. "We're two of us, and we're thirsty. And let's have some lights in here!"

A light clicked on immediately on the wall to their right. In its triangular beam they saw a young man in a shiny white shirt which was billowed and buttoned at the wrists. He was something over six feet and had a thick black mustache and thin black eyebrows. He was standing behind a bar.

"Just opening up," he said in a tentative voice. "Nobody's usually here so early. You spooked me coming in."

"Carol," Gun said. "Want something to drink?"

"I like margaritas," said Carol.

"Do you have buttermilk?" said Gun.

The man's eyebrows tilted in confusion. "I think so," he said.

"Good. A glass of that, then. And an ice tea chaser."

"Disgusting," said Carol. Gun felt the smile in her voice.

It took the bartender several minutes to get their drinks. He fussed noisily trying to find the crusty salt for the rim of Carol's margarita. He worried that the buttermilk was too ripe. At last he put both drinks on the bar. "Just right," he said.

"An ice tea," Gun said.

"Oh." The bartender scrambled.

"My, you're demanding," said Carol. "Do people always respond to you like that?"

"Anyone would demand ice tea if they planned on drinking buttermilk first," he said. "And no. They don't. Not everyone."

The bartender returned, walking fast. A brown half-dollar stain on the left arm of his shirt told Gun he'd hurried with the ice tea.

"I appreciate the effort," Gun said. He laid a five-dollar bill on the walnut veneer of the bar. "Now I'd like something else."

"Sure." The barkeeper sniffed, wrinkling his nose and making the mustache hop. "What'll it be?"

"A little help. Do you know a guy named Larson, first name of Tig, a county commissioner lives down in Stony?"

The barkeeper looked at Gun, then cautiously at Carol and back at Gun. "I know who Larson is," he said, "but I don't know why you'd want him."

"Probably not for the same reason you're used to hearing," said Gun.

"Fine," said the barkeeper. "Makes no difference to me."

"I'd like to know who Larson's pals were," Gun said. "Who he hung out with in here. And how recently." Gun took a long plug of buttermilk, looking over the glass.

"What, did something happen to him?" The bartender elevated his brow in what Gun perceived to be false concern. "You're talking like he's dead or something."

"He drove into Stony Lake off a cliff, most likely

yesterday," said Carol. She picked up the margarita and took a sip.

"Oh, no," said the bartender, in a tone that affirmed Gun's judgment.

"Who did he like in here?" said Gun.

"I really shouldn't talk about that," said the bartender. "Manager says discretion means my job."

"In this case," said Gun, "indiscretion would be wise."

"That's really true," said Carol.

Gun drank ice tea, put the glass down and got to his feet. He gazed down a five-inch slope at the bartender.

"Actually, Mr. Larson was pretty . . . careful," the bartender said. "You know what I mean. He'd get going with one guy for a long time and they'd be real neat. I'd notice them in here together, maybe once every couple of weeks, sitting together in a back booth. No big thing. Then in probably two or three months it'd be somebody else. Always one at a time, though, as far as I could tell."

Gun stayed on his feet. Carol said, "Who was his last? We have to know."

The bartender looked up at Gun, dropped back to Carol. "A guy named Rutherford, Dan Rutherford. Sort of a new face. I don't think I ever saw him before, say, a month ago. A summer boy. What we call a resort queen."

"Was Rutherford here often?" said Carol. She leaned forward, her hair parting to show the back of her neck. Gun noticed.

"Only with Larson. Hell, they met here. The Friar introduced them."

"The Friar?"

"Yeah, the Friar—this older guy with a circle of hair on top. Like Friar Tuck. I don't even know his real name. Comes in here every few months. He brought Rutherford in, sat him down next to Larson." The bartender grinned. "After that," he said, "it was providence."

Gun sat down on the bar stool. "Rutherford," he said. "Which resort?"

"God, you think Rutherford did something to off Larson?" The man stroked one end of his mustache with the tip of his tongue.

"Nope. Which resort?"

The bartender leaned back against a rack of dark whiskey. He closed his eyes. "The Broken Rock," he said. "I think the Broken Rock. It's just a guess, though. I heard that name once or twice walking past their booth."

"Thank you," said Carol. "We'll go now."

Gun stood up. "Got a phone I can use?" he asked.

Without opening his eyes, the bartender pointed to a wall phone off to the right.

Gun went over to it and dialed information to get the right number. At the Broken Rock a young child's voice came on the line. "My dad's not here now." It sounded like a boy. Hard to tell.

"When will he be back?" Gun asked. "Later tonight?"

"He's here in the morning always," said the child.

"Okay, thanks." Gun hung up and walked back to the bar.

Carol got up.

"Don't you want your margarita?" said Gun.

"Too much salt on the rim," said Carol.

18

As they drove back to Stony the sky darkened around them, turning from hazy white to a steely gray-blue. Carol was quiet and seemed to be watching everything with interest: the low rocky fields; the marshlands, still mostly brown with last year's dead growth; the acres of burned-off woodlands; the mossy tamarack bogs, lush and tropically dark. By the time they entered Stony the sky was low and dense, the air sharp with the smell of rain. At the east edge of town Gun turned into the driveway of Peaceful Haven, the resort where Carol was renting a small cabin.

From the middle forties to the late sixties Peaceful Haven had been a favorite vacation spot of wealthy Kansas farmers who drove into northern Minnesota for the singular pleasure of catching bullheads. If they'd been willing to learn Stony Lake's hidden bays and the contours of its floor, they could have had sunfish, crappies, northerns, and walleyes, but most of them preferred to stand evenings along the T-shaped docks and cast into the shaded water beneath over-hanging elms where the bullheads lay, twitching their long whiskers.

By the early seventies the older generation of farm-ers was starting to stay home summers, and the younger generation was going elsewhere. They pre-ferred the newer resorts, the big flashy places with their live bands and tennis pros and saunas. Before long Peaceful Haven was just half full on the busiest weekends, and the owners—Shep and Mary Skaggs, former Kansans themselves—had no choice but to rent cabins out by the month, to locals. Carol lived in number four, which sat on a rock ledge twenty feet above the lake. It was painted light green, same as the other buildings. A big stone chimney covered one end of it. Gun braked to a stop and let the engine idle. Carol didn't open her door. "We're going to get some weather again tonight," Gun said. "You might want to collect enough dry wood for a couple days, in case this front decides to hang around."

"I don't use the fireplace. There's a little gas burner in my bedroom, and I turn that on if I need to." Carol tapped her lips with an index finger. "In fact, I don't even know how to use the fireplace."

"I'll find some dry wood and show you, then. Won't take long to get a little flame going."

Carol looked at him. "Okay. You make a fire, and I'll make supper. How's that?"

He turned off the ignition and the engine dieseled to a stop. "Deal."

In fifteen minutes Gun had enough dry wood for a week of evening warm-up fires: fast-burning birch, a few half-rotted branches of pine, and some whitened lengths of driftwood, delicately curved and smooth as skin. From the neat stack he'd made on the little screened-in porch he took a high armful of wood and carried it inside. The kitchen was cabbage-colored—

smelled like cabbage too, Gun noticed. He walked into the compact living room. It was paneled with a darkly stained particle board. He lowered his load onto the brick hearth.

"Hope you like cabbage," Carol said from the kitchen.

"Sure. What's it belong to?"

"New England boiled dinner."

"Great," said Gun. It wasn't what he expected. Not from a long-time islander. Seafood, maybe, or something Chinese, Italian. Something international. But boiled cabbage and corned beef? Gun turned from building a pyramid of sticks on the iron rack. Carol was setting the table. She was facing away from him. The backs of her legs looked smooth and tan, her waist narrow. As she bent forward to adjust her silver, she tipped her slender hips up and to the right, and beneath her reaching left arm Gun could see the push of her breast against the loose cotton shirt. Then she straightened and walked to the stove with just a little twist in her stride.

When the food was ready they moved the kitchen table into the tiny living room, and there, with the fire crackling and throwing shadows against the wall, they ate quickly and in silence. Gun wanted to say something to Carol about how nice this was, how for the first time in his life he was enjoying the taste of cabbage, even the smell of it, God help him. But he was also thinking of Mazy. He wasn't doing her a lot of good here.

From the west came the first rumblings of a storm, and from out on the water the sad cry of the loon, an airy high-low wailing. They finished eating and Carol said, "I understand how you're feeling, Gun. I'm a parent too. Here, help me"—she stood suddenly and took hold of one end of the table—"let's get the table back in place and sit by the fire awhile. We've earned it, haven't we?"

Gun helped her with the table, then knelt at the hearth. A chunk of smoldering pine had fallen off the iron rack.

"Time you learned about me," Carol said. "I already know about you. And not just from that god-awful biography that came out when you retired."

"Unauthorized."

"Right. Anyway, I got the inside story from Mazy."

"Great."

Carol fell into one of the stuffed chairs and crossed her ankles on a wooden footstool at Gun's side. Gun laid several splintered pieces of birch onto the red and white coals, leaned down and blew a steady stream of air until a flame began to flash up from the coals and lick at the new wood. He remained in a catcher's crouch before the fire.

"Aren't you going to sit down?" Carol said to Gun's back.

"In a second."

"I'll start with the inauspicious beginnings. Livingston, Montana, rancher's daughter, sister of four brothers, model child until the age of sixteen." She uncrossed her ankles and tapped her toes together. Her feet were nearly touching Gun's elbow. He reached over and took one in his hand.

"Fire feels good," Carol said. "Hand, too."

"So. Sixteen."

"I decided Montana was no place for a woman with ambition," Carol said. "Didn't want to end up a rancher's wife. So I talked my parents into letting me spend my last year of high school in California with an aunt."

Gun gave Carol's foot a squeeze and stood from his crouch, moved to the chair beside her. The fire was snapping and breathing, sending out orange sparks which the chimney draft sucked away. The thunder had been getting closer, and now a jarring crack shook the cabin. At the same instant a shot of lightning exploded at the living room window. For a moment the inside of the cabin was bright as noon, then it was darker than before, and quieter, until the first large drops began to strike the roof. Soon the rain was coming hard.

Gun waited for Carol to go on. He watched her profile in the fire's uneven light.

"The next few years, I don't know how they got by me so quickly. Bad decisions are great for speeding up your life. I graduated from high school in San Diego, started college there, got through the first year, and then along came this guy who knew everybody. He told me if I went to Hawaii with him I'd be a model in six months. I went. In six months he was gone and I was looking for a job. Too proud to go home, of course. I started at the *Honolulu Advertiser,* ground floor, writing obits. They're habit-forming, you know. I still write them. This afternoon, for instance. You're bringing Tig up from his car, I'm writing the poor guy's eulogy in my head."

"I don't want to hear it right now," Gun said.

"No. Where was I?"

"The guy left you and you got a job."

"Right. After Stan the First—he was the man of many promises—I met Stan the Second. This one was just the opposite, said practically nothing, Mister Clam, and no promises. Out of gratitude for that I married him." Carol stopped. The rain on the roof was letting up.

"And you had a child," Gun said.

"Yes. Michael. He's twenty now, studying in California. You'd like him."

"I bet I would," Gun said. "What happened to Stan number two?"

"Stan number two found his dream job and dream girl. When I married him he was going to school at the University of Hawaii to be a park ranger. After Michael was born, he graduated, got a job in Redwood National Forest. I waited in Hawaii while he went on ahead. But instead of getting the call telling me to pack up the baby and fly to California, I got a call asking for a divorce. We were together a year."

The rain had stopped and the low rumbling was moving off to the east. The wood in the fireplace had turned to gray ash.

"And for the last twenty years I've been learning journalism and saving to buy my own paper. I won't give you a play-by-play of that."

"Another time," Gun said.

Neither spoke for several minutes. The skies quieted and the rain stopped. Carol laughed softly. "You were really something to watch today. You know that? Diving off the cliff into the water, bringing up Larson from that car?" She bit at her emerald ring. "Something bothers me, though. I don't know how to put it. It was almost like you were . . . enjoying yourself out there today. Am I wrong?"

"Look, Carol." Gun pushed himself up straight in his chair and placed his palms flat on the corduroy-covered arms. He drew a long breath and blew his lungs empty. "It's been a long hard day."

"I know," said Carol, nodding. She looked quickly at the fireplace, then back at Gun. "Does it have to be over?"

"I need to go home, get cleaned up," Gun said. "And you've got to go over to the newspaper office tonight."

"It's only nine-thirty," Carol said.

Gun leaned toward her and picked up her hand. He slowly traced around it with a big index finger, then replaced it in her lap.

Carol smiled. "There'll be another time."

Gun stood up and rolled his shoulders. He bent down and kissed her on the forehead. "I'm glad you said that."

19

He drove home in the dark with the windows down, letting the storm-cleared air wash the inside of the truck. He thought of Mazy, of who she was and why. He tried to think of Tig Larson and brought up only the sight of nipped-off fingers. He remembered how Carol had stood on the bluff that afternoon, looking for him down in the freezing water, the wind snapping at her hair. Then the noise of the wind in the cab took thinking out of his mind and made the trip home as easy as sleep.

There was a solitary letter in his battered mailbox. One he should have thrown away, would have any other time. But tonight the logo of the smiling child next to the return address caught at his brain and made it remember.

The messenger had arrived at Gun's home less than a week after the World Series. It was Gun's Series; his three home runs and ten RBIs in seven games had sent the Cardinals sulking and earned him Most Valuable

Player. He'd celebrated with Amanda and Mazy a few days, taken them to Michigan's Upper Peninsula for salmon. It was Indian Summer on the lake, a rare sixty degrees, and three-year-old Mazy scouted the beach, her long baby curls platinum in the sun. Amanda dressed in too many sweaters and kept her pretty chin pointed at Detroit. They went home early.

Gun was still unpacking when the door bell rang. He waited, not wanting visitors. It rang again. Amanda and Mazy were out, getting groceries. Gun went to the door.

He said his name was Rudy and he had something to deliver from a Mr. Cheeseman.

"Who's Cheeseman?" Gun asked. He had a hard time not staring at Rudy's face, his eyes. The left was normal, but the right had an iris like a little green sequin. It swam in the white.

"Businessman. Import-export," Rudy said. He grinned and slipped a long yellow envelope from the breast pocket of his suit coat. "Has a very big interest in baseball, loves the game. Sends this as a gift."

"Can't take it," Gun said, stepping back and starting to swing the door closed. "I don't know any Cheeseman, and I didn't do anything for him."

Rudy took a step forward and put a hand on the door. "You did, Gun," he said. "You really did. And Mr. Cheeseman appreciates it. And he won't appreciate it if I come back and the delivery isn't made. He'll butcher my ass and bake it up with an apple." The strange eye sparkled, and Gun believed him. He took the envelope, tore it open, and tilted a check for $35,000 into his hand.

"Can I tell him you said thanks?" said Rudy.

"Tell him I'll see him."

"That wouldn't be the best, slugger. Just spend and enjoy. You earned it." Rudy turned on a shiny black heel and left.

It had taken Gun half the afternoon to find Cheeseman's import basement in downtown Detroit. He'd gotten the name of the company off the check— he wished he could remember it now—and checked for a local address in the Yellow Pages. He parked the Lincoln he was driving then out in front of a moldering brick office building, dropped a dime in the meter, went down some steps a flight below street level.

Now, smoking Prince Albert at his kitchen table, Gun couldn't bring up the name on the door. Something or other Ltd. Something African, it must have been, because that's what Cheeseman dealt in. He'd gone inside expecting dimness and cement and saw instead a set from the *African Queen,* banana plants bursting under grow lights, red and blue parrots preening in miniature palm trees, a family of taxidermied cheetahs at play among the greenery. Somewhere a reel-to-reel tape played a loop of screaming birds and hissing night bugs. A fat man in shorts with a watering can said, What can I do for you?

Gun said he was looking for a Mr. Cheeseman, and the fat man sized him up, recognized the World Series MVP and smiled as though thinking of a pay raise. "Mr. Cheeseman just happens to be here," he said. "You're a lucky customer. He spends most of his time in his East Coast offices." He led the way through hanging vines past two jackals and a small gorilla, and showed him a walnut door, then disappeared into the jungle like Tarzan.

Gun knocked, then went in when there was no answer. An even fatter man, maybe fifty and charging toward coronary, sat behind a metal desk. He was talking quietly into a black telephone. He didn't even bother with a call-you-later, just put the phone in the cradle when Gun came in. He stood up, and his hard round face gave off the slightest blush of pleasure. Or,

Gun thought, maybe it was just the exertion of standing.

"Friedrich Cheeseman," he said, putting out his hand. "And you, by God, are Gun Pedersen." Gun shook the hand, warily. It was a strong hand.

"Pedersen, I'm happy you came. I've watched you hit for years, and I think you're an artist. Besides, you hit in the clutch—and those clutch hits practically doubled my net worth in Reno last week. I've got a casino there. I'm indebted to you."

"Listen, Cheeseman—"

"On the other hand, Gun—may I call you Gun?— I'm sorry you came, because I know what you want to do. Rudy told me you'd be around sooner or later, probably sooner, and it'd be my guess as a businessman that you've got my check there in your wallet and you're just aching to hand it back to me."

"It's in my shirt pocket."

Cheeseman chuckled. "Old Rudy. Got a bitch of an eye problem, but can he judge character." He sat back down behind the desk and motioned Gun to a leather chair by the door. "The thing is, Gun, that I reward people who deserve rewards. Doesn't matter if they did it for me or for themselves; if somebody's got something coming, I like to see them get it."

Gun put a hand to his shirt pocket.

"Please, don't do that. You're concerned about dirty money, I see. What a wonderful example for our children. Let me tell you, then, that the particular check you're carrying—those thirty-five thousand specific dollars—came directly from the import section of my business. Stuff I bring over from the dark continent and sell—granted, at a markup, but legitimate all the way." Cheeseman's eyes were gray as a warning. Gun sat quietly.

"You know, I've visited African tribes where it's considered an insult to return a gift. It's bad luck, like breaking a mirror. I don't think either of us needs any bad luck. There's plenty out there already."

For an answer Gun stood up, leaving the check in his pocket, and opened the door.

"You're one sweet hitter, Gun," Cheeseman said, smiling now. "I hope we'll see each other again."

"I doubt it," Gun said, and left.

He wondered awhile what to do with the check. Rip it up, send it back to Cheeseman via mail, put it in a drawer and forget it. In the end he sent the whole chunk to a children's fund in Missouri. Mazy had a pen pal there. Now Gun heard from Missouri twice a year: *Thanks for your past generosity.*

This letter was no different from the rest. He crumpled it and hit the wastebasket on the first try, banking it off the refrigerator.

He woke at three A.M. to the sound of an elephant blaring a high-pitched alarm. In his dream he had approached it from behind, a rifle in his hands, and the animal had turned slowly, red eyes ablaze. Gun sat up in bed and immediately identified the sound: the double-trunked birch outside his window, sawing away in the wind. He lay back down and shut his eyes.

At the tricky border between sleep and consciousness he came into the sensation of standing in a boat on a clear lake and looking into the depths. Way down on the sandy bottom he saw the check for $35,000 from Friedrich Cheeseman. The check said Kudu Club, Ltd. Higher up, in the middle depths, was Lyle Hedman's stuffed elephant, its heavy legs treading water. And higher still, floating just beneath the surface, was the list of Hedman's investors Carol had described to him. He couldn't make out the names.

He lay still and told his thumping heart the connection wasn't likely, not likely at all. All the same, it was common knowledge that Lyle and Mrs. Hedman took an annual trip to Reno—Friedrich Cheeseman's stomping ground. How farfetched was it to think Cheeseman was the man Lyle was working for? Or working to please?

Tomorrow I'll find out, Gun said to the darkness. Tomorrow, he thought, then fell back into dreams of zebras and lions and hyenas laughing.

Cheeseman's number was unlisted, and no one at the Kudu Club's home office in Reno admitted to knowing anything about any development project in Minnesota. One man, a marketing vice-president and the fifth person in Gun's tag-team conversation, said, "Minnesota? Yeah, nice town—stopped there once on my way to Chicago."

Gun hung up and dialed the number again, asked for customer service. A honey-voiced woman named Camille came on the line and Gun told her his name was Lyle Hedman. He complained that the mounted elephant he'd bought from them was getting saggy in the belly. She asked how long ago he'd purchased it. He said he couldn't remember. Ten, twelve years ago maybe. She went to look it up, then came back with the verification Gun was after.

"Yes, eleven years ago, Mr. Hedman. And the invoice was signed by Mr. Cheeseman himself. It was the very first elephant he imported, according to our records. I'll pass you along to Mr. Anders, he handles these repair matters."

"Thank you," Gun said, and hung up.

So, Hedman and Cheeseman were acquainted. It was time for another chat with Lyle.

He looked up the number and dialed it. No answer. Probably the whole damn clan was out for a happy morning swim. Gun hung up, went to the cupboard to find breakfast. Hedman could wait, and in the meantime Gun meant to learn all he could about Rutherford.

The morning sun was bright as Gun drove along County 13 toward the Broken Rock resort. He knew he'd met the owner of the Broken Rock, but couldn't bring a face to mind.

Six, seven years ago he and Jack had stopped in after fishing Tornado Lake, eaten hamburgers at the little bar and grill located in the same low building that housed the resort office. Poor burgers, Gun remembered now, and Jack had made a point of telling the cook.

More recently he'd gotten a phone call from Billy Stanton, an old minor-league buddy who was vacationing at the Broken Rock. That must have been four years ago, maybe five, one of those back-to-back summers of high water. Billy had driven over to Stony at Gun's invitation and taken some swings against the iron arm. No resort owner in that memory.

Gun made a photograph of the place inside his head. The long brown windowless office and store, the dinky yellow cabins, the grassy slope down to the weedy shoreline. Nothing clicked. Then, as he rounded a curve that bordered one of the lake's reed-filled bays, a landmark came into view. It was split in half vertically and looked like the daddy of all watermelons, halved and petrified. Above it was a sign that read BROKEN ROCK RESORT, SINCE 1941. Gun's brain gave a nudge and yielded the answer.

Fourth of July, 1981. Gun was asked to throw out the first pitch for a softball tournament in Emersonville, a small town just south of Tornado Lake. For some reason he accepted. He threw the first pitch that day to a chunky guy wearing a white uniform with a split-boulder logo on the chest. Across the back were letters spelling out HEDMAN PAPER COMPANY. That man was the owner of the Broken Rock. Gun visited with him for a minute before the game started. Listened to him, actually. The guy was a talker. Tried to impress Gun by claiming to be a "close acquaintance" of Lyle Hedman. What the hell was a close acquaintance?

He parked the old Ford in front of the building and walked inside. It was the same as Gun remembered it: dark and low-ceilinged, with a bar straight ahead, a little grill off next to the bottles, a door marked OFFICE to the left. Through an archway to the right was a game room with pool tables, pinball machines, and video games blinking like idiots. On the other side of the game room around a corner would be the little grocery store where resort patrons could load up on beer, pop, hot dogs, and Rolaids.

Gun stepped up to the bar and pressed the button on the silver countertop bell. It took about three seconds for the office door to swing open. Same guy. His shoulders were wide and sloping and bent forward in a muscled hunch. His head was large, his face dark with whisker shadow, his nose exceptionally small.

"Well, Gun Pedersen!" he yelled. "Yeah!" and stuck out his hand. Gun shook it. "Been a while. Too long. How've ya been? You don't look any different than the day we played catch. You remember. July the Fourth. What year? Believe it was nineteen hundred and eighty-one. Have a seat, Gun, have a seat. I'll get you a beer, on the house. Damn, it's good to see ya again. Siddown, siddown, please."

Gun sat.

The man touched the tips of his fingers against both Gun's shoulders and shook his head. "Goddamn," he said, "I'll never forget that one you hit at Met Stadium in 'sixty-five when you beat the Twins in the ninth—middle of August, I believe it was, Kaat was on the hill and he threw a big curve and you swung from the heels"—here the man took a big, loose imaginary swing that spun him clear around and landed him back next to a plastic rack of beer mugs—"and boom! Second deck. Bobby Allison out in left didn't even bother to turn around and watch it come down. Shit. I was sitting up there that day and didn't get the ball. Some hog with a glove reached out right in front of me. Should of busted his face." Now the man picked up a mug from the rack, lifted it, and wiped his sweaty forehead with a hairy wrist. He smiled. A lot of pink gum showed above his upper row of teeth. "What'll it be, Gun? We got Miller, Pabst, and Mick."

"Miller."

"Miller it is." He drew a mugful by feel, smiling and keeping his eyes on Gun. "There you be."

"Thanks," Gun said. "Now, what's the name?"

The man looked hurt for a moment, then brightened again. "Slacker, Larry Slacker. You know, we met at the softball—"

"I remember you well," Gun said.

"Yeah, I thought so. Saw the recognition in your eyes right away. Damn"—he popped a fist into an open palm—"I'm gonna just take a little beer break myself, if you don't mind." He was already filling a mug with Miller. Turning his face away from Gun, he coughed. The cough had a bad sound.

"I'd like it if you joined me, Larry," Gun said.

"Hey!" Larry pulled up a high stool and sat down across the bar from Gun. One bead of sweat clung to his short nose, several to his wide chin. He was still grinning. He took a deep raspy breath. "So tell me, what brings you out this way, Gun? Fishin' Tornado, I bet. And let me tell you, my people've been catching crappies the size of dinner plates without so much as getting in their damn boats. Hell, they're catching 'em off the docks with angle worms. Never seen anything like it in the twenty years since I bought the place, but of course—"

"Reason I'm here," Gun said, "is to talk to you."

"No shit." Larry looked puzzled and pleased. He took another breath. His lungs didn't sound good at all as they filled up.

"I need some information about one of your recent guests."

"Oh?" Larry expelled his chestful of air.

"A guy named Rutherford. From Minneapolis, I think. I want his address."

Larry went bottoms-up on his beer, then set down the mug. "Sorry, Gun. But I've never even known anyone by that name, that I remember. And I do make an effort to get to know my people. That's an important part of the business. You want your people to get the feeling like they're part of a family. Kind of like a team, you know? *You* must understand that, Gun—team spirit and all. It's what I try to do here at the Broken Rock."

"I think you're forgetting one member of the team, Larry. His name is Rutherford. He was staying here about a week ago. Think harder."

"Look, Gun, even if he was staying here—and like I said, I'm pretty damn sure he wasn't—but even if he was, I couldn't tell you a thing about him anyway. My files are confidential. Lots of pretty important folks have passed through here over the years, and they go home and tell their friends about the Broken Rock. So I can't just start passing out addresses and such to anyone that asks—not that you're just anyone, Gun. But you gotta see my point. I start giving out stuff like that and pretty soon I'm going to lose my reputation and the resort goes to hell. *You* must understand, Gun. You're a guy that knows the value of privacy." Larry's face was running with sweat now. He drew himself another mug of beer. "Your brew okay, Gun? Hardly've touched it."

"It's fine," Gun said. He could see Larry was going to take a little persuading. It wasn't fun to push a guy who was so eager to please. Especially one with gravel in his lungs. Gun took a sip of beer, which was getting warm.

"No hard feelings, right?" said Larry. He was still grinning, but not the same as before. His grin stopped above the mouth.

"Of course not," said Gun.

Larry sighed, then finished his second beer, taking the bottom half of the mug in two swallows. He shut his eyes and shook his heavy face back and forth. "Gun," he said, "that same game I mentioned before? With the Twins? Your homer in the ninth? Wasn't there a helluva brawl in that game? Benches cleared, if I remember right."

"Yup." Gun got up from the stool and walked back to the door, six paces away.

"Hey," Larry said. "Leaving already? Thought you might tell me about that little scrap with the Twins. And your beer . . ."

Gun shut the inside door, blocking out the sun and making the room even darker than before. He threw the dead-bolt lock.

126

Larry stood up. "Whatcha doin' anyway?" he said.

"I'm going to tell you about that brawl—and believe me, it was one of the best ones I was ever in. Then you're going to go into your office and get Rutherford's address for me." Gun walked back to the bar.

"Gun, really, I can't . . ." Larry coughed and shook his head.

Gun stood before the bar, then leaned down with his elbows so that his face was even with Larry's. "I spent most of my time on Earl Battey," Gun said. "Remember him? He was about your size, maybe a little huskier. Anyway, we ran into each other between the pitcher's mound and third base and he hit me pretty hard in the gut. So I threw a straight left into his nose and roundhouse right to his ear. And you know, he didn't go down. So I hit him hard as I could right here"—Gun touched a finger to a spot right below Larry's breastbone—"and damned if he didn't go down. And stay down."

Larry stepped back, one arm lifted in conciliation. He wagged his face and the perspiration flew. "Gun, I'd like to help you. But I—you see—I told someone I wouldn't say anything about this Rutherford guy."

"Hedman, right?"

Larry's eyes said yes.

"Don't worry about Hedman right now, Larry. Worry about me."

Larry nodded slowly, then went into the office. He came back promptly with a manila folder. Gun took a pen from his pocket and copied Rutherford's address on a scrap of paper from his wallet. "Thanks, Larry," he said. "You've done the right thing."

Larry was sitting again, and nearly finished with another beer. The energy had drained from his face.

"What do you know about Rutherford?" asked Gun. "What did Hedman say?"

"Hedman said he was a partner of some kind who needed to keep a low profile. That's it. Zippo. I don't know shit about the guy. Not a piss-poor thing."

21

It was four o'clock that afternoon when Gun eased the pickup into the shade outside Jack Be Nimble's and tapped a *Let's Go* on the horn. He could still taste the Prince Albert tobacco in his mouth from the cigarette he'd smoked while talking to Mazy on the phone three hours ago. She'd called just as he was about to leave for Minneapolis. Now he'd wait until tomorrow—until after Tig Larson's funeral—to go visit Rutherford.

Jack stepped outside, pulled the oak door shut behind him and checked to be sure it was locked. Out from behind his bar Jack looked even shorter than his five-three and less like a stone Roman than a shaved bear with perfect posture. A poorly shaved bear. His arms were black and his curly chest hair reached halfway up his neck and ended in a crooked razor line.

He climbed into the truck and slammed the door. "You didn't say much, Gun," he said. He held his chin down against his chest. It was his way of frowning.

"*She* didn't say much either. Just that she had some news for me. Good news. And that I should come out for a visit because she wanted to tell me in person."

"Something about the land, I suppose."

"That wouldn't be good news, would it?"

Jack shook his head. "I'm not sure why you want me along on this deal," he said.

"I want you along because I don't trust my own judgment," Gun said. "About Mazy, and the Hedman kid. Finally I get a chance to see them together, and I want to read things right. Trouble is, I might see only what I want to see. I'm counting on you to be more objective."

"Don't know if I can be."

"Try."

At the edge of the Hedman land Gun and Jack found the iron gate open and unguarded. Jack said, "I'm sure they only do this for relatives."

Lyle Hedman was waiting on the front step of his grass-roofed house. He was standing in a relaxed slouch, his thumbs in the belt loops of his tan, creased trousers, his shapeless face bright with self-satisfaction. Gun and Jack left the truck beside one of the unlit gas torches and walked over to him.

"Nice of you to come, Gun. And you brought a friend." Hedman stepped forward and shook Gun's hand, then Jack's. "Jack LaSalle," Hedman said. "I don't forget names or faces."

"Lyle Hedman," said Jack. "Neither do I."

Hedman laughed and gave Jack a friendly slap on the shoulder. Then he whistled, and Reuben came loping up from the lake. The dog's reddish-brown hair was flattened with water. He shook himself at a safe distance before padding over to his master. "Good boy, Reuben," Hedman said. Reuben whined. He rolled his yellow eyes up at Gun and shot lake water out his nose.

"Where's Mazy?" Gun said.

"She'll be along shortly. Prettying herself up, I imagine." Hedman curled his tongue down over his bottom lip. "I think maybe she and Geoff have been upstairs, napping." He shook his head the way people do when they're remembering the old days, and chuckled. "Come on, let's go 'round back to the gazebo."

Gun and Jack followed Hedman and Reuben. The gazebo wasn't a gazebo at all, but a green safari tent the size of a two-car garage. Two of its walls were canvas, the other two mosquito netting. Inside was an aluminum camp table. Scattered around were half a dozen director's chairs in green, red, and yellow. A sterling ice bucket on the table held a long-necked bottle of champagne. Gun thought, This doesn't look good at all.

"Pull up a seat," Hedman said.

The men arranged themselves in a generous triangle. A woman came in with a tray of champagne glasses. "Thanks, Mona," said Lyle. "I'll pour." Mona left, and Hedman stood to take care of the champagne. Before he'd finished filling the glasses, Lyle's wife and Geoff and Mazy came out the back door of the lodge and walked toward the tent.

Mazy looked all right—but then, she always did. She wasn't one to show what she was feeling. Gun watched her closely. Her walk seemed normal and she held her chin high, almost defiantly so. She wore Levi's and a white V-necked T-shirt. As she entered the tent her eyes darted back and forth, from Geoff to his plump mother. Gun stood up. He and Mazy hugged each other. He could feel the tension in her arms and back.

Mazy said, "How are you, Dad?"

"I'm fine."

"I'm glad you came." Mazy was holding Gun's

hand now, gripping it like she didn't want to let go. Her eyes were serious. Her voice lacked the huskiness she'd developed as a tomboy and never outgrown. "We've got some good news for you, Dad. Geoff and I do."

Damn, Gun thought.

"Here," said Lyle Hedman, pushing a glass of champagne into Gun's hand.

Geoff put his arm around Mazy's shoulder and guided her away from her father. Hedman Senior handed out champagne. The group stood in a loose circle. Mazy looked at the ground between her feet. Geoff looked grinning at his father.

"Okay, let's hear it," said Lyle Hedman, lifting his glass toward his son. Mrs. Hedman, clutching tightly to her husband's arm, imitated his movement.

"Yeah," said Geoff. He brushed a lock of hair out of his eyes and glanced apprehensively at Gun. "Really, I think Mazy should tell her father. I think that's what she wants." He turned to Mazy.

She lifted her face and met her father's gaze. "I'm pregnant," she said.

Gun thought, The hell you are.

"Early February it looks like," Lyle said to Gun. "You're going to be a grandpa."

Geoff threw back his glass of champagne. Mazy looked into hers. Hedman cried, "To a healthy, sturdy, baby boy," and flourished his. Hedman's wife took a meek sip, eyes fluttering. Gun and Jack didn't lift their glasses. They stood with their legs planted firmly apart, bodies tilting stiffly forward like sailors in a gale.

"Gun, Gun," Lyle said, spinning a circle in the air with a thin hand, "now is the time to drink to the health of our first grandchild, not the time to think politics or business or any of the——"

132

"Let me get one thing straight here," Gun said, looking at Geoff. "You knew about this and didn't tell me."

Geoff's Florida tan was turning splotchy. His eyes implored his father for help.

Lyle Hedman said, "Gun, this isn't the nineteenth century."

"I'm talking to your kid," Gun said, pointing a finger at Lyle but not taking his eyes from Geoff.

"Well, ah, yes, Mr. Pedersen," said Geoff. "You must understand, though, that Mazy and I didn't want it to be like this, not at all."

"Gun," Lyle said. "They're old enough to make their own decisions."

"And to speak for themselves. I want to hear from Geoff, not you. Straighten me out on something. How do you know Mazy's pregnant when you only started seeing each other two weeks ago?"

Geoff shook his head quickly. "We would have liked this to be different, but this is how it turned out. We were seeing each other several months before you knew anything about it, in Minneapolis. Considering your position, it was difficult to say anything."

"Dad." Mazy looked up from the ground. Her voice was back again, husky, almost confident. "Geoff's telling the truth." She looked away toward Hambone Bay, large and round and turquoise, with a small green island in the center of it. "Dad," she said, "we want you to know something else. If it's a boy we're going to name him Gun." She kept her eyes on the lake.

"Now, that sounds like a wonderful idea," said Lyle. He set down his glass of champagne and made a soundless clap. "Gun Hedman."

Jack laughed. Mrs. Hedman let go of her husband's arm and strode purposefully to Mazy. In a clipped monotone she said, "Mazy and I are going to do some shopping this afternoon. We'd better get started." She took Mazy's hand. Mazy allowed herself to be led from the tent.

"Gentlemen, please," Lyle said. "Sit down. Now that the women are gone, I want to talk a little business. Overdue business. Gun, it's high time I put your mind at ease about a few things." Hedman sat down lightly in a green director's chair. Geoff stood listening in the door of the tent. "Please," Lyle said, indicating the chairs on either side of him.

Gun and Jack stayed on their feet. Hedman coughed, then whistled for Reuben, who'd been lying in the shade just outside the tent.

Hedman crossed his legs. "I'll come right to the point, Gun. First, I couldn't be more pleased that Geoff got such a fine wife, though I can see you're less than enthusiastic about the match. Okay. Second, things couldn't have worked out better regarding Loon Country. Mazy was quite happy to offer her land for the project. In fact, it was her idea, not mine. She wants to see the economy thrive here in Stony, and she wants her children to be financially secure. She's really a very bright girl."

Gun said, "You said you'd get to the point."

Lyle bowed his head slightly. "Here it is. Mazy wanted to ensure that you wouldn't be adversely affected by this thing. She insisted that your cabin and the forestland surrounding it be fenced off to guarantee you won't be bothered. You'll have two hundred and fifty feet of lakeshore and plenty of woods. It's all arranged."

"Plenty?" Gun said. "How much is that?"

"Ten acres."

Jack said, "Hey, that's great. You're coming out ahead on this deal, Gun. You get to keep your cabin, and if you ever get tired of being out there all by yourself on that big plot of land, you can just walk across your backyard and check into the Radisson Stony for a weekend, take in a nightclub act."

In the truck Jack said, "She was nervous, sure, but what can you expect. I think she's doing one hell of an acting job. If you ask me, the whole troop of them was acting. I'd just like to know what they're holding over her head."

"Use your imagination." Gun shifted down and turned the Ford into Jack's parking lot. He turned off the engine, which made its usual kicking departure. "I've always been able to see through her before," he said. "Or thought so."

Jack opened the passenger door. "Another thing. Hedman's got the land he wanted, right? So if this thing's a charade, why keep it up? You can bet he's had Mazy sign the papers. How long are they going to make her play the game?"

"Simple enough. They make her play along until after the referendum Tuesday. If she's playing."

"What about after that?"

"I don't know."

"Then we better move before Tuesday."

"We will."

22

"I want to see Jim," Gun said. The woman behind the glass window was half hidden by a glossy philodendron vine.

"Dr. Samuelson, you mean."

"His name's Jim." Gun reached through the window and held the vine aside in order to get a better look at the person he was talking to. He didn't know her. She had gray hair piled up on her head like a corn shock. Her eyes were huge behind thick lenses. Her white name tag said EDNA.

"Yes, well, Dr. Samuelson's not here," she said.

"Where is he?"

"And he won't be back until . . . let's see"—she reached for a black notebook and riffled through it—"until July fifteenth. He's in Europe, you see."

"I'll bet he just left too."

"As a matter of fact, yesterday."

"Of course," said Gun. Damn convenient. "Look, I need a favor, okay?"

Edna's eyes blinked carefully, like the eyes of a serious fish.

"I want you to check your files for me," Gun said. "Last week Samuelson examined my daughter. Mazy Pedersen . . . Hedman."

"I know who you are," Edna said with a formal nod.

"I want to see that report."

Edna touched her fingertips to the top of her gray cone of hair, as if to be sure it hadn't toppled over. "I'm sorry, but I simply can't do that. Policy."

Gun was still holding the green vine out of Edna's face. He said, "It's important that I see that report. If it makes any difference, I've known Jim, Dr. Samuelson, for a long time. He wouldn't say no. I'm sure of it."

"With all due respect, Mr. Pedersen, it's not my decision. It's policy."

"Tell me," Gun said, making an effort to modulate his voice, "is there any way I could contact Samuelson? By phone, today?"

Edna shook her round face from side to side. "Not by phone. But there's a forwarding address."

"No," Gun said, and he let the vine drop back in front of Edna's face. As he turned to go he caught sight of a small orange dot. He leaned down toward the window for a closer look. Sure enough, affixed to a brown purse that was hanging on a chair to Edna's right was an orange button that said VOTE NO ON LOON COUNTRY.

"Edna," Gun said. His face was right up to the window opening.

She looked up from an appointment calendar and pulled back, startled.

"It's wrong to follow policy sometimes," Gun said. "Would it help if I told you that this has to do with the

Loon Country mess? Please let me see the file on my daughter."

Edna touched her fingers to her hair again and hummed a short low pitch, her lips pressed tight. Then she stood and went to a row of gray file cabinets.

Samuelson's report verified Mazy's claim. Pregnant. Gun wasn't surprised. Do it right or not at all, he thought.

"Thanks," he said, returning the file to Edna. "One other question. Do you have any idea when Dr. Samuelson made his vacation plans?"

Edna shrugged. "He and Mrs. Samuelson go every year about now. Have for a long time. Most people know that."

"Do they use a travel agent?"

"Fredericks, I believe."

By the time Gun reached Fredericks Travel it was five o'clock. The office had closed early. Gun drove home and phoned Paul Fredericks at the golf club. Samuelson had made his plans early. Six months early.

Which didn't mean much, Gun told himself. He was sitting at the table, smoking. None of it really meant anything. For Lyle it would have been a matter of talking things over with Samuelson, making an offer as sweet as was necessary, and promising the good doctor that Mazy would later claim to have miscarried. The doctor's reputation would remain untarnished, and he'd be able to spend an extra week or two on the Riviera. No one the wiser. At least that's how Gun preferred to think it must be. "None of it means a thing," he said to the kitchen table.

He put out his cigarette in the square glass ashtray. Then on impulse he stood up and went into the spare bedroom, took down an unopened bottle of Johnnie

Walker Red Label and walked down to the lake. He untied the Alumacraft and stepped in.

The surface of the water was smooth, and Gun followed an imaginary line across the width of the lake, past the four cluster islands straight toward the inlet, the mouth of Woman River. He followed the center of the narrow river for a mile, passing beneath the lake road and coming eventually to a second bridge. He ran the bow up onto a low grassy bank and took a small pair of battered binoculars from his tackle box. He climbed out of the boat and up the grade to the roadbed and walked to the middle of the bridge.

Ahead of him the river widened into a sprawling marsh: hundreds of acres of rushes and cattails, dun-colored mostly, but starting to brighten here and there with new shoots of green. The main channel of the river wound through the marsh like a string of bright blue yarn.

Through the binoculars Gun spotted it right away—the dark brown hump rising several feet above the tops of the rushes. It was a good half mile away and probably a couple hundred yards from the main waterway. There were other muskrat houses in the swamp, thousands of them, but this one was by far the largest. For some reason that Gun didn't understand, the little animals chose to build their palace in the same exact spot every year, without fail. Gun had driven by every summer to check.

He returned to the boat and motored upriver half a mile. He cut the engine. Using an oar he poled the Alumacraft straight into the heavy marsh. In some places the water was four or five feet deep and had a solid bottom. In others it was shallower, but had a bottom so soft and boggy he was able to drive the long oar right up to its handle. The rushes were thick everywhere. It was slow travel.

The sun was nearly gone when he finally ran out of water. The dark mound was still twenty yards off and he couldn't pole the boat any closer. With the bottle of scotch in one hand, Gun lifted his right foot out of the boat and tested the surface of the bog. It felt solid enough to walk on. He swung his other leg over the side and let his full weight come down. The crust gave way. Gun fell against the bow of the boat and the bottle cracked on the gunwale.

"Aw, damn," he said. The amber liquid streamed from a crack that jagged down the glass, neck to base. He lifted the bottle and shattered it against the aluminum hull. He pulled one foot out of the muck and took a long high step away from the boat. The smell of rotting swamp stung his nostrils. The bog gasped and sucked at his feet.

In twenty slow steps Gun was sitting on the firm lodge of reeds and mud and cattails. He watched the light fall low in the sky, then seep down behind the dark hills to the west.

Next morning he watched the sun come around again. It was the second sunrise he'd watched from this spot, and it wasn't as spectacular as the first. Ten years ago he'd been less sober, and the glaring colors had looked deeper than blood.

23

Stony Lake Community Church was located at the once-picturesque corner of First Avenue and Lake, where the city crew had recently amputated from the boulevards a total of thirteen veteran oaks stricken with wilt. The stumpage invalidated the lush post-cards once produced by the Stony Chamber of Commerce, which featured a traditional brick church, grandly overfoliated in leafy oak, and the silver-lettered slogan, "We visited Stony Lake. Why don't you?" Now, on a June day bound for an unseasonable ninety degrees, Gun sat on one of the stumps and watched well-dressed men and women file into the church. They were going to bury Tig Larson.

"Going in, Gun? Or are you just going to flatten your ass on that stump all day?" Jack LaSalle was not dressed for a funeral. He was wearing jeans and a tight, dark blue T-shirt that outlined concrete pectorals.

"It'll be warm," said Gun. "Yup, I'm going in.

Don't know if the good shepherd will let such a wolf as you in, though, what with such a tender flock." He nodded at Jack's attire.

"He shouldn't worry. I'm going in to pay my respects, but I can't stay. Left a sign at the bar that says Back in Fifteen Minutes."

"Be nimble, Jack."

"Ha."

People were already sweating inside. The forty pews—two rows of twenty with an aisle down the center—were nearly full. Men used hankies against their brows. Women fanned themselves with blue-bound hymnals. Reverend Barr was somewhere out of sight. Tig Larson was in a closed walnut box at the altar, the coolest man in the house.

After a wait of some twenty minutes the Reverend Barr opened a narrow door near the pulpit and ascended into it. All hankies and hymnals were quieted as he gripped the stand and glared out over the gathering. He stood stiff for a minute. Then he said, "There's a terrible reason we're here today." Barr let his eyes drop to the podium. "A favored member of this body lies before you," he said in a low, emotional tone. "And his death is one that could have—yes, should have—been prevented."

Gun felt something like a drop in atmospheric pressure as forty pews' worth of bodies inhaled and held it. The barometer's dipping, he thought. Change in the weather.

"All of you know me," said Barr. "You know I'm not a judgmental person. Not one to lay blame on anyone's shoulders. The Lord is slow to anger, quick to forgive, and I try to follow His example."

There were nods around Gun as listeners bowed to the vinelike strength of Barr's voice.

"But this is needless waste, this terrible end that our

142

brother Tig Larson brought upon himself. Needless. It makes me angry, and I'm going to tell you why."

Get to it, Gun thought.

"Tig Larson was a brave man," said Barr. "A brave man who stood up and looked reality straight in the face, and in turn decided to face others and tell them what he'd seen."

Concentration was plain in the squints of the mourners. Sweat tracked down their temples, unmopped.

"The week before he died," Barr said, "Tig came to my study with a problem. He said he'd been doing some research. Research into an issue that mattered to Tig in his heart of hearts."

Barometer's dropping, Gun thought. Watch those clouds.

"There was only one thing more important to our friend Tig Larson than his beloved lakes, trees, and sunshine. And that was the health and wealth and wisdom of his fellow Stony residents. As a man in a position of leadership, Tig felt it dearly every time one of our locals lost a job or missed a meal," Barr said. He swept the pews clean with a slow staring stroke. "Our brothers in the timber business, feeling hard times. Our resorters, feeling a slowdown in the tourist trade. Tig Larson was a man of compassion, and in the end he decided to compromise one ideal—a natural paradise—to aid another—a prosperous county and community. That was the problem Tig came to me about. He was afraid of the reaction that his public support for the Loon Country development would arouse."

Gun felt a dribble of sweat running like an ant down his neck and reached back to dab it away. Should have dressed like Jack did, he thought, and left just as fast. Humidity's rising.

"And this is the part," said Barr, "that makes me angry. It seems Tig was right to be afraid. When he came to me, I said, 'Don't worry, old friend, they'll understand. You just go out there and tell them how you feel.' And that's what he did. Not that it was easy for him. But he made a hard and honest choice, and at the public hearing he made his voice heard. And do you know what happened then?"

The barometer fell out of sight. Gun wondered if people were breathing.

"I'll tell you what happened." Barr stood up tall in the pulpit and his sweaty face glowed like Moses' on the mountain. "Tig went on home. He went home to take the rest of the day off, to recuperate from the meeting. And then the phone began to ring. It rang time after time, and every time Tig answered it, and every time it was a local resident, and the residents were mad because of Tig's decision. They called him things. They called him a turncoat. They said he'd betrayed his duty!" Barr slapped the pulpit with both hands.

Lightning and thunder, Gun thought.

"And worst of all," Barr went on, "they never let him explain that they were the very reasons he'd changed his mind." Barr paused, letting the vibrations he'd produced sink into the plaster. "They were hungry, and he offered them food. They were naked, and he offered them clothing. But they rejected all, and that rejection was more than Tig could take." Barr stopped, took out his own hanky and wiped the rage from his face.

There it was, Gun thought. The storm, brief but effective. He relaxed in his pew and waited for the rainbow.

It came. "I don't know who among you made those telephone calls," Barr said softly. "But I know this.

When you go off to decide for yourselves what we're to do with this poor famished paradise, you'll be thinking of Tig Larson. I want all of you to search yourselves, and if you're part of the problem"—he nodded almost imperceptibly at the walnut box—"then I encourage you to become part of the solution. We can never justify a man's death, but maybe we can make it seem less tragic. We all have one vote to cast. Mine's going for Tig Larson—one last time." Barr was done. He bowed his head to pray.

Gun missed the prayer. His attention was on the reverend's bowed head, which was, as he'd noticed before, bald on top with a ring of gray all around. Before it had meant only that Barr was losing his hair. Now it reminded him of someone else. Friar Tuck. *The* friar.

People lost no time in getting out of the thick church air. Gun stayed behind until the pews were empty, then walked back past the pulpit and entered Barr's study through the narrow door.

The reverend was leaning back in a fat leather chair, his clerical collar off, his white short-sleeve shirt open at the neck, his eyes hidden under a damp washcloth. Gun's entry had been quiet.

"Very nice talk, Friar Barr," Gun said.

Barr snatched away the cloth and jerked forward in the leather chair. "Polite to knock," he said, with low control.

"So you were at Larson's home, then, right before he died," said Gun.

"What?"

"When all those angry people called him up. Were you there listening, or did he just stop by here on his way to the bluff and tell you about it?"

"I don't know what you're getting at, Pedersen,"

said Barr. "Tig called me up that day. I was here at the office. He told me what was happening. The next day—well, you know. You found him."

Gun walked over to Barr's desk and leaned his knuckles on Barr's Calendar of Holy Days. "Do you know what I think? I think you could fill a cathedral with the amount of crap you just unloaded out there. I think you know damn well why Larson drove over the edge."

Barr leaned back again, placing the tips of his fingers together in a pastoral repose. "And what about you, Pedersen? What do you know about why he went over the edge?"

"I know he didn't go home to wait on the wrathful citizenry," Gun said. "I know he didn't change his stand on Loon Country because he was worried about resorters. And I've got a very good idea about why he did it, and when I know for sure, a lot of people are going to be very disillusioned about the sacred leadership of Stony." Gun removed his knuckles from the desk and stood straight over Barr. "Afternoon, Friar," he said, and walked out of the study.

"Don't call me that," Barr called after him, less control now in the rising voice. "The title's Reverend. Reverend Samuel Barr!" And he sat back in the leather chair, mouth open, staring at the ceiling.

24

The next morning Gun rose ahead of the sun, took his swings and swim in the creamy dawn mist, then went inside and made the sort of breakfast he figured could stoke a man through difficult tasks. In a large stainless pan he dropped two chunks of smoked Virginia ham, searing their sides on high heat. When they were sizzling he cracked four eggs onto a cast-iron griddle and cooked them sunny-side up, spooning over fat from the ham. He ate the eggs soft-yoked, with slices of cracked wheat bread. Then he went out on gravel to the lake road. On Highway 71 he turned south and headed for Minneapolis.

Rutherford's street address was 1637 Griswold Avenue. Gun didn't know the area, but he had a map—the one from Larson's Buick, drip-dried, stiff and pocked but serviceable. It placed Rutherford in a residential area near the University of Minnesota. A student maybe, Gun thought, earning some tuition money through furtive grips with a northern politi-

147

cian. It was possible. The Reverend Barr, Gun knew, had left a Twin Cities church to come to Stony, though Gun hadn't heard why. Could be that Barr had known Rutherford there and offered his special services to Hedman as a tool against Tig Larson. Barr certainly could have been "the Friar" spoken of by the bartender at the Back Entrance—who'd know him, thirty miles south of his parish? Gun squinted his left eye against the rising sun as he drove and tried to think of other men he knew with Friar Tuck halos. There weren't any. But then, he stayed at home a lot.

Ninety minutes south of Stony the lakeside resorts and motels, even the mobile-home parks, began shedding their overpainted, hardscrabble siding for aged wood and cedar trim. Bay windows swelled from clean cabins. The trees grew in ranks, hand-planted, and the grass was clipped right up the bark. This was about as far as most of the city people were willing to drive on their weekends off, and the city was starting to show. Gun stopped at a small red café with a mug-shaped neon sign and had a cup of coffee.

"You been in here before," said a man with a shiny scalp. He wore a white apron with a jumping bass iron-on.

"Nope," said Gun.

The man eyed him down the counter. "You used to play football," he said.

"Nope," said Gun.

"Well, shoot," said the man, wiping a glass with an apron. "Had you pinned for the guy used to play tackle for the Lions in Dee-troit. You sure?"

"I live up near Stony," Gun said. "Had a place there for a long while."

"Well, shoot," said the man.

"Sorry," said Gun. He dropped a dollar next to the empty cup and left.

The temperature had risen enough for Gun to be

uncomfortable with only one window down. He leaned over and reeled open the passenger window, then upshifted and drove with the wind crackling in his ears.

So. If Barr really was the Friar, then it made sense to guess that Larson had killed himself to avoid blackmail. Acting as matchmaker, Barr might have introduced the commissioner to Rutherford, then conspired with friendly Lyle to catch the action in a camera lens. A discreet presentation at Hedman's lodge, complete with black-and-white glossies, could have shown Larson the grave error of his conservationist ways.

Gun felt in his shirt pocket and came out with his tobacco pouch and papers. He spread a paper, sprinkled, and rolled a cigarette on his knee. Chances were Rutherford would have been warned—a call from good old Larry Slacker, probably, or from Reverend Barr right after Gun's post-funeral intrusion. Damn, Gun thought. Rutherford was probably in Miami by this time. Walking the beach until the referendum was through, the land overturned, the megamall open, and the condominiums doing a pleasant trade in time-sharing blue-suits. And Mazy, permanent daughter-in-law to Lyle. Gun put the cigarette in his mouth and felt in his shirt pocket. He hadn't brought matches.

When the sun was at the top of the sky and turning the highway to water ahead, Gun turned on the radio. A sign told him he was eighty miles from Minneapolis, near enough to pull in WCCO. The Twins were playing the Detroit Tigers, game one of a doubleheader. Herb Carneal announced the score, three to one Twins, and the inning, fourth. Gun shook his head.

Rutherford might be gone, then. *Here, kid, go take a month in San Francisco.* But there would have to be some evidence of a connection, if there was a connection. If Rutherford was out of town, Gun figured, he'd wait until dark and pry open a window for a look around. He may have forgotten matches, but a four-cell flashlight rode under the seat, next to the Smith & Wesson.

Allan Anderson was pitching for the Twins. With one man out in the Tiger fifth, Anderson walked a batter, then hit another. The hometown crowd buzzed worriedly. Herb Carneal remained placid. Anderson struck out the next two batters. Gun thought about Mazy and needled the speedometer to seventy.

Running through it in his brain, Gun couldn't believe she was pregnant. It only magnified the reason he hadn't wanted to believe in the marriage in the first place. Mazy had never shown any interest in Geoff. She didn't hate him, except for a brief stretch after the camping incident. He simply had not mattered to her. He was a thing in the background, an annoyance from the past.

Thirty miles from the Twin Cities the Tigers were batting, top of the ninth, one out. Three to two, Twins. Anderson gave up a single, then walked a man, and Kelly went to the mound. Herb Carneal announced a new pitcher, one of the Twins' anonymous relievers. Gun smiled; he could see it as if he were there in the on-deck circle, working his hands into the handle of the bat, watching the new kid whipping in his warm-up tosses. Smelling pine tar, waiting, feeling the coolness inside. Ready. Herb Carneal gave the batter's name and Gun listened as the first two pitches went wide. On the third pitch Gun thought *swing* and the batter did, sure enough, the ball snapping over the radio and into the space between left field and center. A gapper. Gun turned up the sound, two runs scoring under Herb Carneal's dispassionate voice. Four to three, Tigers, and Gun thought: a happy ending.

He entered Minneapolis in late afternoon and felt the temperature rise by ten degrees. The old cement towers and the wider, glass-sided new ones trapped the air and held it in the streets. Gun steered the F-150 into a vacant lot and rattled Larson's city map across his knees.

It took him forty minutes to locate Rutherford's house; 1637 Griswold was large and light green and peeling, with the kind of narrow lapstrake siding preferred by the wealthy in the 1930s. It did not look wealthy now.

The house stood next to a four-story brick building with chipboard tacked up over the windows. On its other side were tall, full trees, their lumpy trunks ringed with orange paint. The house itself was in a dark permanent shade.

Gun street-parked directly in front of the house, behind a round-edged silver Thunderbird. If this was Rutherford's car, he was doing all right for a student. Gun doubted that he lived alone. The place was too big. A rental probably, shared with other students. Gun squinted at the dark windows. He was right, Rutherford didn't live alone. Gun could see the movement of several people in the low light, bodies busy with some sort of action. He couldn't tell how many there were, and he didn't want to speculate on what they were doing. But as he watched, a shiny surface flashed for an instant, and Gun immediately recognized it. It was the sheen of a baseball bat, still new with varnish, and it reappeared again and again, swinging downward like an axe.

25

The street was quiet as Gun burst from the Ford, vaulted the front end of the Thunderbird, and ran through Rutherford's yard like it was center field. A few steps from the door he remembered the Smith & Wesson, but he didn't stop. If Rutherford was taking those baseball-bat blows, he needed speed before force. Then Gun was through the door and twisted screws and hinges were zinging through the darkened room, and two men in light polo shirts stood over a crumpled-up bloodied figure. Too late.

The one holding the bat was about six-two, and spread upward from his pencil waist like an overturned volcano.

"The door was unlocked," he said. His voice was low and liquid, full of potential. "You didn't have to mess it up that way."

Gun stood still while his eyes adjusted to the dimness. He was glad the man with the bat had spoken. It meant he was the type who liked to intimidate with his mouth before doing the real damage.

Gun didn't answer. He kept his eyes open, his hands low. He charged.

The guy with the bat wasn't looking for it. He had to pull back his arms for a swing, and Gun's height and speed pushed his hurried blow too high. Gun ducked it easily and caught the man's breastbone with a powder-keg shoulder. It broke his grip on the bat and made a loud crack in the plaster when the man hit the wall. Gun turned and looked for the other one. He was taller and leaner and took Gun more seriously. He moved on his toes like a boxer, fists making circlets in the air. Gun could hear him blowing soft jabs of air through his nose.

Gun didn't dance. He stood on the balls of his feet, heels a half inch from the floor, one foot slightly ahead of the other, and waited. The boxer seemed impatient. He shuffled. Gun didn't move. The boxer's head bobbed side to side across his shoulders, anxious. Gun could hear the first man moving now, probably groping for the bat. The boxer couldn't wait any longer. He sent a lanky jab at Gun's face, and Gun slapped it away with an open hand. Behind Gun the first man rummaged on the floor. The boxer feinted with his left and came in with a roundhouse right, and this time Gun did not slap the hand but caught it in his own and snapped it downward, clenching his jaw as he felt the snap of wrist bones. The boxer screamed and went to his knees. Gun released the hand.

The first man had recovered the bat and enough of his nerve to belt Gun from behind. The blow was vertical, like those Gun had witnessed through the window. It landed on Gun's collarbone. He felt the swoosh of air in his right ear just before the pain.

It was flat and numbing and thick, like being hit from behind by a quiet Kenworth, and the swelling fire of it made Gun feel like he was expanding to fill the room. He locked his knees, fighting blackout, then turned to see what he could do to keep it from happening again.

The man with the bat was breathing hard. His chest was rumbling as he recovered from the effort of the swing. Gun watched from a cloud as he brought the bat back, sighting in, shifting his feet for balance. He saw the man in stop motion: pant, screw his knuckles down tight on the bat handle, spit red on Rutherford's dark carpet. Then he swung.

The action pulled free Gun's sunken reflexes. His left hand shot up, palm open to protect his head. It was like catching a cannonball. Bat met flesh with a cherry-bomb crack, icing Gun's entire forearm in a glow of shock. He closed his fingers and found them encircling the bat. It had stopped cold, two inches from his temple. The attempt made him angry, and he squeezed the bat and ripped it away. He grabbed the man's shoulders and pushed him into a silver-framed print of *Guernica,* breaking the glass.

"You're working for Hedman," Gun said. "Tell me all of it. Now."

The man looked down at his buddy, who was rocking his wrist and sobbing on the floor. He looked sullenly at the walls. Then his eyes went to the dark door of an adjoining room, and at the same moment Gun heard the soft squeal of floorboards. He dropped his hold and spun, saw two guys dressed in jeans and black T-shirts. One was tall and skinny and carried some weapon Gun had seen once in a terrible movie on a coach flight: two smooth sticks joined at the ends by a short chain. The wood was lacquered black, shiny. The other guy was short to medium, empty-handed, and had a high-school mustache on his lip.

"You jerks took your time getting in here," said the guy Gun had let go.

"We been havin' a look. Little faggot didn't keep much stuff around, did he?" The tall skinny one looked at Gun and shook his head. He was holding one of the sticks loosely in his right hand so the other stick dangled free, and now he started a slow wrist motion that made the dangler do unhurried circles. "You be one large sonovabitch," he said.

Gun pointed at the tall man's sticks. "I saw one of those in a movie once."

"Yeah?" A smile.

"Bad movie."

The guy with the ruined wrist had dragged himself over near the door. "How fast can you kill that bastard?" he said, in a voice not soft enough to hide the sniffles.

"Pretty fast," said the guy with the sticks. Gun saw the swinging wood accelerate to a blur, saw a sudden metal gleam in the hand of the short kid, felt his arms yanked back by the guy he'd gone and let go of. His collarbone felt wrong, weak. There were too damn many of them.

"Nice thing about the nunchuks," said the stick swinger, "you get them going like hell, you can't even see what hits you," but then the front screen door crashed in and Gun *could* see the nunchuks, could see them perfectly as they came free from the long skinny hand and flew at the ceiling, splitting the plaster. He heard the muffled *whup* that straightened the tall guy up like a post and the second *whup* that brought spray from his neck. There were two more people in the room now, holding short black pistols with long black silencers. The short kid was dead on his face, *whup*, and the boxer with the broken wrist hadn't even had time to get up off the floor. The guy that had been holding Gun's arms was out in front now, on his knees.

"No, don't, I got to pray," he was saying to the

155

pistols, but one of them came forward to rest between his eyebrows. Gun turned away. *Whup.*

In the quiet Gun had his first chance to look at his rescuers. If that's what they were. They came toward him now, not talking, one wearing an unspringlike red stocking cap, the other in camouflage fatigues. There was a quick bitter scent of spent shells and copper.

The man in the stocking cap touched Gun's elbow and pointed to the kitchen. The other man, Gun realized, the one in camo, he'd seen before. It was the eyes. The right eye. The iris was abnormally small, stranded like a little green island on a large white globe. Now the eye winked at Gun.

Gun said, "Hi, Rudy."

Rudy nodded and almost smiled. He led Gun through the kitchen and opened the door for him. A van was backed up to the steps. Gun climbed in and took the chair Rudy offered, a padded office chair bolted to the middle of the floor. Rudy and stocking cap stashed their guns in compartments under the carpeting of the van's floor and sat on benches along the windowless sides.

"Tell me, Gun, how is it everybody remembers my face?"

"A gift and a curse, I bet." Gun nodded at Rudy's right eye.

"How you been? Your hair turned white since I seen you last, what, twenty years back now."

"After the series," Gun said. He remembered his confusion that day, answering the door and finding this man standing there, unmatched eyeballs and a comedian's grin. "So tell me. What's Friedrich's stake in all this? Must be a big one, you folks seem serious."

"It's Freddy now, part of the makeover. But he'll want to discuss it with you himself."

"So we're on our way to see him."

Rudy nodded.

"Don't tell me we're going to Nevada."

"No. Not even leaving town. Freddy's got a temporary office here. I think you might like it too." Rudy looked toward the front and called to the driver, "Almost there?"

The driver answered with a hard right turn. Gun felt the van strain against a steep incline, then level off and slow to a stop.

"Here we are," said Rudy. He reached into his chest pocket and said, "You'll need this." Before Gun was aware of what Rudy had thrust into his hand, the van's double doors flew open and before them, hulking beneath the city's skyline like a buffalo in a field of dazzling stars, was the hump-backed Metrodome. Gun looked at the ticket in his hand.

"In the mood for a game?" Rudy asked.

"I never did like warehouse ball," Gun answered. "Let's go in, anyway."

26

The wide cement corridor had T-shirt booths and TV monitors and too many decibels of crowd noise. Rudy stopped at a food stand, bought three brats and handed one to Gun. "That way," he shouted, pointing.

Passing a gate, Gun had his first glimpse of the field. It didn't look like a ballfield so much as an illustrator's rendition of one. The perspective was all wrong. Everything was too green, too distant, too small. The players were little plastic men on a shampooed rug.

Rudy knocked on a gray door in the corridor. It opened and Gun was looking at Friedrich Cheeseman, who put out his hand. Gun wasn't ready to take it. Not yet.

"A pleasure, again," Cheeseman said. Behind him was a clear Plexiglas wall, and beyond that the playing field.

"I hope so."

Cheeseman ushered Gun inside and dismissed

Rudy with a wave of his manicured hand. His face was lined and leathery and round as an old-fashioned catcher's mitt, but now as he smiled, it turned oval with happiness. He hadn't changed much over the years—maybe put on a few more pounds—but something was different. Gun couldn't tell what.

"But it is a pleasure. Please, sit down." Cheeseman gave Gun a stuffed chair next to a table loaded with cold cuts, crackers, vegetables, and fruit. "Nice view, don't you think?" he asked, sitting down.

Gun nodded and took a bite of his bratwurst. Below, Kent Hrbek hit a sharp single to left, scoring Puckett from third.

"What about these guys!" Cheeseman cried, tilting his head toward the playing field. His manner was easy. Gun might have been an old friend Cheeseman watched games with every week.

"Good bats," Gun said.

"Damn right. A little help in the right places and they could contend. I think I might buy them."

"Pitching'll cost you some."

Cheeseman smiled. "I've dealt in arms before." He laughed, then turned back to the game and swore as Bush struck out to end the inning.

"Friedrich, what's going on?"

"Freddy. Call me Freddy."

"Part of the makeover."

"I've come a long way, Gun." Cheeseman sighed, pouting a little. "I'm respectable. I'm clean. I don't even throw shadows anymore, you know? Me twenty years ago, me now. Two different men. Nobody's got anything on me. No embarrassing friends anymore." He winked. "Except a few in prison."

"I don't care about all that."

"I know, but you do need to know what I've become. It's important that you trust me. You see, there was Friedrich, and now there's Freddy. Freddy's on the up and up."

"And before—the man I met was Friedrich?"

"Friedrich turning."

"All right."

On the mound one of the Twins' white hopes pumped and fired. The pitch smoked into the dirt right at the ankles of the left-handed hitter, who backed away and glared.

"You're right about the pitching, Gun," said Freddy.

"I'm ready to hear what you've got to say."

"But you haven't even thanked me yet. My driver phoned and said you had your hands full over in that queer guy's house."

Gun waited. Freddy wasn't a man to be rushed, you could tell by the serene set of his eyes, the way they held to things like a pair of strong hands.

The two of them sat silently through the rest of the sixth inning, then Freddy stood from his padded chair and stepped right up to the Plexiglas, pressed his hands to it and bowed his head for a few seconds. His shoulders were rigid. Then he turned and crossed himself, let his arms drop to his sides, leaned back against the glass.

"Gun, I had nothing to do with the ugliness, at least not directly. Gospel truth." His eyes and mouth were steady. "Let me start from the beginning, straighten things out for you."

"That would be nice."

"You're familiar with my import business."

"Your treasures from the heart of darkness." Gun remembered the outlet in Detroit where he'd gone trying to return Cheeseman's check. "Banana plants, stuffed cheetahs, I seem to recall a gorilla."

Freddy smiled. "I did some bigger things too. An

elephant once in a while. You may have seen one of them."

"That's how you met Lyle Hedman."

"Yes, my casino in Reno. We got to talking one time, oh, ten, eleven years ago now. He's one of those guys with idealized notions about everything. You know the type. And he came on to me all chummy, full of too many movies about," he smiled, "the family. Asking all sorts of questions, pretending my life is a dark secret that I'm gonna share with him one of these days. So I humor him. I mean, the man's gonna drop a load into the wheel tonight, I wanna keep him happy. Then it turns out he's into Africa, so I'm able to milk him coming and going. That elephant, for instance. I get five hundred percent markup on it and send Lyle home happy as a worm in a shitpile.

"So Lyle, anyway, he keeps coming back every January. It's the games, sure, but more than that. For him it's a chance to rub shoulders with a gangster. Maybe he'll get invited to an initiation, or maybe I'll want him for a blood brother. Maybe we'll burn each other with live cigars." Freddy shook his head and laughed. "Then last year he had a proposition for me. A good one too. He had drawings, market research, seventy percent of the money already lined up. I can see it's a sunny idea, this Loon Country, so I tell him I'll put up twenty-five percent, contingent on the political go-ahead. It's just my word, no papers, nothing. He trusted me. We smoked Havanas and I nicked my finger on a diamond lapel pin, dropped blood into a burning candle. Gave the poor bastard a thrill. You should have heard my wife Margie howl after Lyle left that night."

Freddy indulged himself with another chuckle and turned to see what the crowd was humming about. A collision at home plate had left two men sprawling, the baseball trickling away toward first base. The runner pressed himself to extended push-up position and stood. The catcher rolled over, sat up, and threw his glove in disgust. "God, that Gaetti's a bull," Freddy said. "I don't care if he *is* born-again, the man can play."

"What do you know about my daughter?"

Freddy put up a hand, his eyes still on the field. "You're getting ahead of me," he said, then turned. "Look, Lyle Hedman is a foolish, impressionable ass. What went wrong is this. His imagination got the better of him. I took a trip north to see his—your lake, Gun. This was a month ago now. I saw that swampy land he'd bought and I told him I didn't like it. Told him I don't throw my money away for fun, like those little insects that buzz out to Reno once a year. I said if he didn't find a suitable place for fantasyland, I was going to be very upset. To put it simply, I played the role he'd cast me into, and I played it hard." Cheeseman took a breath and fogged the Plexiglas blowing it out. "It backfired. Didn't think the little man had the testosterone to swim into the deep water."

"Don't know if that's what it took," Gun said. "He was probably crapping his pants, wondering what you might be planning for him."

"Yeah, well, I'll tell you—what he did took me by surprise. Setting up your county commissioner with that fag you were checking up on this afternoon. I'm still not sure how he did it. Don't know who the runner was. My man picked up the trail at a queer bar, traced Rutherford back here to the city via that rundown resort on Tornado Lake. When I heard about the suicide, I put a watch on Rutherford's house, figuring Lyle might get nervous, try to take him out. I don't need any messiness in my life right now, Gun.

It's taken me fifteen, twenty years to squeeze myself into this respectable life I'm wearing, and I don't want a dumbass like Hedman screwing it up. And he won't. Nobody's gonna know I ever had anything to do with his project. There's no legal connection. His word against mine."

"So where were your boys when my head was getting busted?" Gun asked.

"Lunch break," Freddy said, laughing. Then his face went cold. "Hell, a month ago when I was up to see Lyle I didn't even know you had property on the lake. Hedman never said anything. First I heard about it was my man telling me Hedman snatched your girl."

"Do you know where they've got her?"

"I don't. But you can be sure Lyle's got nothing good in mind for her. He's gone this far, and now he's got to go all the way. He didn't realize that when he started. The little fish never do." Cheeseman turned toward the game again. It was the eighth inning and Berenguer was trying to hold on to a one-run lead, throwing bullets, enough of them off target to keep the Detroit hitters away from the plate and swinging with cautious respect.

"You can't tell me anything more about Mazy?"

Cheeseman shook his head. "Wish I could."

"I want to believe you," said Gun. "Don't know if I should."

"We're ex-big-leaguers, Gun. That's how I see it, both of us. And to me there's a brotherliness about that. I respect you a hell of a lot and I don't want to see you—and certainly not your daughter—get jerked around." It occurred to Gun that the gray of Freddy's eyes was different this time. Before, when they had met in the sixties, his eyes had been the color and dull sheen of nickel, hard, protective, unchanging. They seemed to have brightened and deepened into a softer grayish-blue. It was like the difference between the false sky of the Metrodome and the sky outside. Maybe the man was simply wearing tinted contacts, but Gun found himself convinced that Freddy Cheeseman was speaking the truth.

". . . so I asked myself," Freddy was saying, "What would I want if I were in your shoes, if Mazy were my daughter—and the answer was easy. I'd want to take care of it myself. I'd want the man, and I'd want the man's kid, and I wouldn't want anyone else in my goddamn way."

"Which means you're out of it. You don't want anything more to do with Hedman."

Freddy smiled.

"But say, you did tell him good-bye, didn't you? He had a pretty sore face last time I saw him."

"I heard about the blackmail stuff and had my boys pay him a visit and deliver a message. Then I heard about your girl, and I broke things off completely. He's all yours now."

"Thanks."

"Don't be kind to the man," said Freddy, and he turned back to the game.

27

Gun awoke feeling dirt-dried from sleeping in his clothes. He was lying on top of the dark wool quilt that was his bedspread, with a bolt of ripe yellow sun batting him in the face. He opened his eyes and sought the clock without turning his head. Six forty-five. He'd had two hours sleep after the drive up from Minneapolis. It would have to be enough.

Sitting up, Gun felt his collarbone begin to beat like a bass drum where the bat had connected, and he reached for the wall to steady himself. His left hand was stiff as a plaster cast. When the throbbing eased off he stood slowly and stripped to his shorts. The shoulder looked bad, with a black bruise starting at the base of his neck and swelling in a proud arc to where the arm attached. Gun faced the mirror and forced the arm to move. It hurt, but he didn't feel the screaming pain or internal scraping that meant a broken bone. He made the arm rotate, a small circle, then a large one, and diagnosed a crack. The hand he paid less attention to. It was his glove hand, still tough from two decades of catching hard-hit and hard-thrown baseballs. Nothing had ever hurt his hand for long. He closed it into a fist, and the pain shot his memory back a few hours.

Rudy had dropped him off, and he'd approached Rutherford's house with caution, his only idea being to reach the truck and head north before anyone decided to pay Rutherford a visit. It was dark but a bright amber streetlight showed him the house, undisturbed, the front door hanging aslant. Apparently no one had gotten suspicious. It seemed strange, a planned murder and four more spontaneous ones, carried out in the middle of a simple, mundane neighborhood. People all around, Gun thought, and not one of them aware of five dead bodies hardening in a living room right here in a house they'd all walked past a thousand times.

It was getting late. Gun got in his truck, put the key in the ignition. He looked again at the house with its green peeling paint. A big brown doormat he hadn't noticed before said WELCOME, FRIENDS in script big enough to read from across the street. Gun opened the glove box and took out a pair of fuzzy yellow work gloves. Not skin-tight white latex, but they'd do.

The room was ripe and the floor sticky under his Pony runners as Gun made his way through Rutherford's living room. He remembered tenth grade, reading *The Red Badge of Courage*, when the young soldier looked into the eyes of his first corpse and went witless, tearing through the woods. He avoided the gaze of the scowling dead and headed for Rutherford's kitchen.

Freddy Cheeseman seemed to have the whole Hedman scheme figured out, or most of it. He knew Rutherford had been used to set up Tig Larson, knew Rutherford was headed for Niagara in a breadbox because of it. But he didn't know it all. "Don't know who the runner was," he'd told Gun. Gun had the runner figured to be Reverend Barr, the thin Friar, but he wanted to be sure.

He was sure after a ten-minute search of Rutherford's ample kitchen. Even with a near-useless left hand he was able to sort rapidly through a stack of mail on the counter, bills and letters and postcards, nothing with the Stony postmark. He found what he sought in a drawer beneath the telephone: a thin red address book. Samuel Barr was penciled in between Back Entrance and Broken Rock resort. Gun slipped the book in his pants pocket and stepped with care to the front door. No one said anything. He propped the screen into a more likely position on his way out.

With bacon thawing and coffee ticking on the stove, Gun broke routine and walked in his underwear down to the lake. No hitting practice this morning. A cracked collarbone deserved a day of rest. He walked to the end of the dock and dove without breaking stride, parting the water with his hands, welcoming the anesthetizing chill of Stony Lake. He did a slow sidestroke, resting the sore half of his collarbone. He floated home on his back. When he reached the shore he ducked once under, then rose dripping into the sunshine. A thin pinkness had begun beneath the bruise on his shoulder. His left hand felt stiff but capable. He glanced at the roofless stone boathouse. Later, it would provide therapy.

Breakfast was Wheaties, crushed in the bowl to hasten sogginess, a dull but functional Breakfast of Champions. Gun ate quickly, then dressed in jeans and a wide red sweatshirt. He looked at the phone, thought of Carol's black bangs and green eyes, and went out to the F-150.

It was time for confrontation, Gun thought as he

drove to the Hedman estate. Past time, overdue, and calling in the loan. Carol had asked him earlier why he didn't put the questions straight to Hedman's face, the questions about Mazy and Larson and Rutherford. Evidence, he'd answered her then, he needed evidence. Well, he had evidence now. Larry Slacker had been shaken loose, and Rutherford had been shelled apart. And there was the new topography of Gun's shoulder, rising up like a tender knoll, big as a slab of sod. That ought to merit a piece of Lyle's busy morning.

When Gun drove up to the iron gate, the jumpsuited guard stepped back a pace from the bars and smiled. He wasn't the same guard Gun had spanked earlier.

"Hello, Mr. Pedersen," said the guard. He was taller than the last one, and muscled like a TV wrestler.

"I want to see Hedman," said Gun.

The guard raised his arms in a sorry gesture. "Mr. Hedman isn't here," he said. He was still smiling.

"You might as well open the gate," Gun said. "The easy way or the hard way, I'm going to see him."

The guard hiked the .38 on his hip. "Pedersen," he said, "you used to be a hero of mine."

"I'm glad."

"Used to dread the Tigers' road trips to Minnesota, you swingin' through Twins' pitchers like a wrecking ball. Gave me a thrill, though—I saw you hit three homers off Perry and Kaat in a doubleheader at the Met once."

Gun waited.

"Thing is, though, I don't watch baseball now, and you don't play it. You don't pay my salary either, and Mr. Hedman does. So I wouldn't let you in, even if he *was* here." The guard shifted his shoulders once, as if he were uncomfortable under the jumpsuit. "But like I said, he's gone. Took the family. Took the dog, even.

Caravan of Jaguars, the old man's, the kid's, the wife's. Damn."

Something about the guard made Gun believe he was telling the truth. The part about the Jaguars. He said, "Where did they go?"

"Come on, Pedersen. I'm a security boy, not a vacation counselor. They don't tell me where they go. They just tell me to watch this gate"—he reached out and slapped an iron bar— "and make sure that people on the other side of it stay there." The guard showed Gun a sudden grin. "Another thing," he said. "When Hedman *is* here, I don't deliver notes."

"You're a smart boy," said Gun. He got into the Ford and rode out on Kenya Drive, aiming south when he hit the highway.

Driving with his bruised hand out the window, Gun tried mapping his limited options. Time was spinning ahead too fast. He'd delayed confronting Hedman until he had some ammunition, and now that he had it, Hedman was gone. With his wife and his kid and his ill-gotten daughter-in-law. The polls would open at eight A.M. Tuesday, and it was Saturday already with the sun heaving up toward noon. Gun goosed the Ford south on County Road 2. If the Hedmans were anticipating him, the Reverend Barr probably was too. But it wouldn't hurt to look.

Barr lived in an off-white house of European stucco with craggy slopes and ivy crawling a fieldstone chimney. Like Hedman's place, it was invisible from the road. Gun nearly overlooked the black rural mailbox imprinted with domino-sized capitals: S. BARR. The thin gravel drive took him through a tall lilac hedge and into a meadowlike yard. He pulled the Ford up in front of the broad brown front door and left the engine running.

The door had a window and a fat bronze knocker. Gun used the window first. He beheld a small, wallpapered entry with hanging coats showing from a dark closet door. A snaggle of wire hangers had been tossed onto a high-backed Shaker chair, and a yellow plastic dog-food dish was upside down on the hardwood strip floor.

The knocker made a sound like a locker being slammed. Gun gave it three sharp beats and waited. No one was home. He gave it three more, and the bronze horseshoe came off in his hand. Gun walked to the back of the house. There was a long narrow yard, framed at the edges by yellow-blossomed caraganas. Across the yard opposite the house was a cubelike building of matching pale-faced stucco, with square-paned windows. It looked like the servants' quarters in a TV miniseries about nineteenth-century England. Gun squinted through one of the windows. The place was a garage, and it was empty. An oil drip pan sat in the right stall. The floor was swept. Gun could see the swoop and straight lines of a ten-speed bicycle under a sheet of thrown canvas. A strip of twisted gold fly tape hung from the ceiling, bugless.

The sun said it was noon. Gun left the bronze knocker in the reverend's mailbox on the way out.

"They took off," said Gun, "every damn one of them." Jack Be Nimble's was cool and smelled of fresh frying grease. Gun had just finished bringing Jack up to date on the Rutherford killing, the Cheeseman connection, and Lyle's quick exit.

Jack chuckled, rubbing his thick fingers over the black crew cut. "Seems you mentioned that Cheeseman guy one time. Didn't know you ran in those circles, Gun."

Gun looked at the empty bar in front of him. He said, "Aren't those things done yet?"

"Should be." Jack rolled away to the kitchen. When he returned he had two long plates with a shingle-shaped burger on each. The buns, full-size kaiser rolls, perched on the meat like decorative cherries. Gun's plate held buttermilk in a beer glass.

"Before," Gun said, "I might have been able to just blow in there and get her out. But I waited too long, and now everybody's gone."

They finished eating with no more talk. Gun tucked a five under his plate and got to his feet. "Wherever they went," he said, "I'm going to find out."

"Tomorrow's Sunday," said Jack. "My day off."

28

By nine-thirty that evening a rack of washboard clouds had slid over the sky, curtaining the bright new moon and promising a black night. Gun, stiff but strengthened from an afternoon roofing the boat-house, used the last of the light readying the old Alumacraft. He removed any item that might rattle or clank: a pair of loose-jawed pliers under the bench seat, a long teardrop-shaped landing net, a tackle box. He untied the anchor from its rope and tossed it on the grass, then coiled the line and tucked it in the bow, leaving one end secured to the eyebolt in front. He reached into the new boathouse rafters and drew out two long bleached oars, oiled the locks until they swung lightly, and laid them in place. At last he pushed the boat into the water, floated her next to the dock, and rocked her with his feet until the gunwales scooped water. There was no noise but the slap of the waves he'd created.

The straight-line route from Gun's to the Hedman

shore was roughly four miles, or about eight minutes in one of the low-slung, high-chaired bass boats that were increasingly populating the lake. In Gun's battered rig, pushed through the dark by a dutiful fifteen-horse Evinrude, it took much longer. At ten-fifteen he was carefully edging past the rocky point that stood out from Hambone Island. Ten minutes later some of the gaslight lamps that lit the Hedman drive were winking through the shoreline trees. Gun idled down and cut the motor. A chill wet breeze made cat's paws on the water. Gun reached into a pocket of his canvas hunting jacket and brought out a black wool watch cap.

The Woman River exited Stony Lake at the southern edge of the Hedman property. Moving parallel to the lakeshore, Gun rowed silently until he could make out the two ghost banks of rushes that marked the outlet. Then he pointed the boat between them and floated in driftwood-quiet on the current.

He waited to land until there was a small thinning in the wall of cattails, then dug one oar into soft river bottom and nosed into the weeds. Through scrub-willow branches Gun could see flaring African lamps, lit for extra security in the absence of the Big Bwana. The wet breeze blew him the sound of the gas hiss. Gun poled through the rushes until the boat thumped the mossy bank, then replaced the oar and stepped aground. He tied the free end of the anchor rope to a reaching hook of willow root, put his toe to the prow of the Alumacraft and shoved. The boat disappeared like a spirit in the sway of weeds.

The main lodge sat on the crest of a hill, perhaps seventy yards distant and fifty feet in elevation from where Gun crouched in the willows. He was wearing the watch cap over his white hair. He also wore the brown canvas jacket, black woolen pants with dark green flecks, and ankle-high leather boots soft with mink oil. He felt like an ad for L.L. Bean, but at least he wouldn't attract any eyes.

It took a murky half hour to reach a small, grass-thatched hut some twenty yards from the lodge. He hadn't yet seen a sentry, though he suspected the night guard would be heavy. He sat down in the black shade of the hut and watched for movements in the gaslit yard. Thank God Lyle traveled with his dog, Gun thought. Last thing he needed tonight was Reuben.

He heard macadam footfalls before he saw the guard. On his stomach in the wide black shadow, Gun's eyes gradually pulled the man into vision. Like the others, this guard wore a light green sleeveless jumpsuit. A three-quarter-sleeve baseball jersey covered his arms against the night. The standard .38 was a proud lump at his side, and a nightstick jumped on a chain at his thigh. The man walked between the lamps on Kenya Drive, headed for the lodge. Gun pulled back behind the hut. He heard the tread of boots on wooden steps, and the *chuck* of keys as the guard let himself in. When he peered forth again, the guard was returning to the porch. A six-pack of silver cans glowed in his grip.

"Hey, Horseley, you big hog!" The sudden voice was as high and thin as a nerve in the air. It was also close. Gun tensed his body, strained his eyes.

"Bondy? Where the hell are you?" The first guard, standing on the porch, bent his neck forward, probing. Yeah, Gun thought, where?

"Sipping the old man's imported reserves, hey, Horseley?" said Bondy, piercingly near.

"Damnit, Bondy, where are you?" yelled Horseley. He set the six-pack on a rattan porch chair and used both hands to shadow his eyes as though looking at the sun.

Bondy laughed. "Horseley, you're a blind man. Right here. The shed." Gun felt the vibrations of the hut as Bondy slapped the other side of it, not fifteen feet away. He rose to his knees and then to the balls of his feet, as careful as if the earth had a ticklish skin.

"Jeez, Bondy." Horseley sounded relieved. "You blended in. Goddamn chameleon. Why don't you get your ass up here and share some of the wealth?" Absolutely, Gun thought. Get it up there.

Bondy made stiff, musclebound noises getting up. He must have been sitting there some time before Gun ever pulled up behind the hut. Horseley picked up the six-pack and sat down in the rattan chair.

"Here's to sudden vacations," said Bondy. He unzipped a beer can and tilted it high.

"Here's to expensive Hedman brew," said Horseley. "The man has taste."

Gun leaned against the dark wall of the hut for the twenty-minute duration of the six-pack. He was in an unfortunate location, since the hut was lit on three sides by the gas lamps. He might shift back the way he'd come, but getting anyplace would take too long. He wanted to get into the lodge, not away from it.

"*Grock,*" said Horseley, belching mouth open, hippo style.

"All gone," observed Bondy, putting his eye to the top of his can.

"More to come," said Horseley. He stood, quite steadily, and let himself into the lodge.

Chilled from staying motionless in the misty night, Gun set a limit. One more six-pack and he'd take action. Forward or backward, but action. He blew a soft sigh and rubbed his palms. He craned for a look when he heard the porch screen swing to. Horseley was carrying two six-packs.

"Bless you, Marse Lyle," said Bondy.

The second six-pack was only a fifteen-minute wait. The guards were doing their best not to let it get warm. While Horseley and Bondy giggled the empties into a twelve-can pyramid on the porch, Gun reached for the layered steel padlock on the door of the hut. Cautiously at first, he rattled the lock against the metal clasp. It made a sound like a squirrel on a tin roof. Bondy and Horseley drowned it out. They were having a belching contest. Gun grabbed the lock as he had Barr's knocker and pounded it against the clasp. He had to do it four times before the sound sunk through the laughter. Horseley put one hand on his gun and the other on Bondy's shoulder.

"Crap, man, did you hear that?"

Bondy grinned a strong imported grin. "Aw, get off it."

"No. Seriously. I thought I heard somebody sneaking around, out by the shed maybe."

Gun knocked again.

"The shed," said Horseley. "Shit. Someone's in the shed, knocking around with the old man's mowers."

Bondy took a step toward the screen door and stumbled over the beer pyramid. The tinkling scramble seemed to tighten their nerves.

"I'm going out there," Horseley said in a beer-amplified whisper.

"I'm right behind you," said Bondy, whispering too.

Gun flattened his back against the wall of the hut and waited. They said nothing else, but Gun could hear the unsnapping of holsters and feel their uneven steps as they approached. The wet breeze sharpened against Gun's face, and the long blue glow of a .38 barrel nosed blindly around the hut's corner.

Gun didn't wait for its owner. He seized the barrel in both hands and jerked Horseley into black shade, the pistol erupting and blowing an orange hole in the air six inches from Gun's left shoulder. The shot startled Horseley into a scream, and for one frozen frame Gun could see the horrified whites of the guard's eyes. He darkened them with a staccato punch to the face and wheeled for Bondy.

Bondy wasn't there. Gun panted quietly for less than a minute before he heard the guard's voice, bleak and sodden.

"Horseley?"

Bondy was close, very close. Gun guessed he was against the adjacent wall, on the corner, too scared to enter the shadow. His finger would be nervous on the .38.

"Come on, Horseley, talk," muttered Bondy. The guard's breath fluttered in his teeth like a moth. "Did you get 'em? Tell me you got 'em, Horseley, this is a damn bad joke."

Gun edged to the corner. He thought, I'm a monster in the dark, boy. Then he curled one hand into a searching claw and flung his arm around the corner. It connected immediately with Bondy's soft sweaty neck, and Gun felt the .38 hit the earth. He pulled the guard squeaking into the shade. He was careful, when inducing sleep, not to hit too hard.

29

It was cool and still inside the lodge. Faded yellow gaslight entered through the frequent wide windows and landed on the hardwood floor in rectangular sheets. Gun locked the door behind him and stood near a window. The pistol shot had been a bad turn; other guards, posted on Hedman's borders, would be on their way. They might waste a little time waking up Horseley and Bondy, but not much.

After a minute the grounds around the lodge were still quiet, and Gun switched on the four-cell beam and flung it around the room. The gray Hedman elephant straddled the couch and leered into the eye of the light. Pregnant goddesses glowed in ivory, fertile forms on ebony tables. Gun didn't know exactly what to look for, some sign of Mazy or a destination, but he knew he wouldn't find it here. Not in Lyle's museum.

An arch framed with leather-laced tusks led Gun into a wide hall with doors to the right and left. The right door opened into a factory-sized kitchen large enough to feed a safari, and probably the elephant. The left door showed only a narrower, carpeted hall, with a sculpted walnut door at the end of it. The door was unlocked. Gun opened it and switched on a light.

The room was no more than a small private cube, covered on the walls with African spears and diamond-oblong masks. A round blue pool took up most of the floor, surrounded by fur-covered pillows of every shape and species. Gun snapped a switch on the wall and the pool roiled up into foam, fogging the air.

"Damn," Gun said out loud. On the opposite wall a long peach nightgown hung from the point of a stone-tipped spear.

Upstairs he located Hedman's monstrous master bedroom, an affair made comic by the presence of two separate single beds pushed against opposite walls. More interesting was Lyle's study, which contained a fat oak desk piled with papers and a well-scribbled calendar. Gun studied the calendar by flashlight: no cities, no flight times, no plans. He tried the drawers. One was locked. It gave under an angled kick, and Gun dug down to the bottom through file folders, newspaper clippings, letters. As he closed it, something rattled. On second look he pulled up a plastic-cased videotape. The hand-printed label said, *The Art of Persuasion*. Gun pocketed the tape, shaded the light, and descended the stairs.

Reinforcements had arrived. In the gaslight a stooping cluster of khaki jumpsuits worried over Horseley and Bondy while several fanned out to points near the river. Evidently they reasoned that whoever jumped the guards took immediate leave, instead of staying around. Gun was glad he'd hidden the boat.

He left the lodge by a dark back door that serviced the kitchen. The sounds outdoors were panicked:

pounding steps searching the bank, face-slapping and grumbling as the two guards came groggily around, quick shouts faintly distorted by breeze. The tiny pointed scent of gas whetted Gun's sense of smell, and dimly across the meadowy slope he could see the shape of a squarish thatched building.

The guest house. If Hedman hadn't held Mazy in the lodge, she might have been billeted there. It was going away from the river, but the gas lamps were fewer here, and so were the guards.

He crossed the meadow in a fast stomach crawl, avoiding the patches of weak light cast by the lamps. Behind him he could hear activity in the lodge, the swearing of sentries. He looked over his shoulder. Windows blinked on, burned in outrage for a few seconds, and were extinguished.

The guest house was locked, but Gun still gripped Horseley's key ring, and he hit it right on the second try. If the guards were sacking the lodge now and came up empty on the riverbank, the guest house would be next. Gun didn't bother to search the first floor. Weren't bedrooms always on the second?

Mazy had been here. The upstairs suite connected two bedrooms with a bath and a kitchen that smelled of spilled champagne. In one of the rooms Gun's flashlight exposed a closetful of clothes, Mazy's size. The bedspread had been yanked in a hurry over humps of blankets. On the stand beside it lay the long red finger of a candle, tipped over in mid-flame, dots of red wax spattered over the wood. Gun searched the drawers of the ebony dresser. They were empty except for a wallet-sized photograph. Gun picked it up. It was a picture of himself.

The other bedroom held less of interest. At least at first glance. Geoff's clothes were squeezed into the closet and dresser drawers, and a long robe hung from a quarter of the high four-poster bed. Gun noticed the bedspread, an African print quilted Minnesota-heavy, made into hospital corners. It looked unslept-in. Then he saw what was lying on top of it.

A single sheet of paper, triple-creased, with letterhead and a few sparse lines of type. Against the dark bed the paper glowed in Gun's beam. He seized it, blessing the conscientious travel agent who'd dutifully sent an itinerary to the travel-bound Hedmans.

They were in Canada. The agent specified that holders of six tickets were entitled to flights via Northwest to Calgary, Alberta. They'd gone yesterday morning, rising west out of Winnipeg, out of his reach. Gun scanned the paper for a return date and came across another piece of information. Only five of the tickets were of the round-trip variety. Someone was staying behind.

A scatter of approaching shouts muffled through the glass made Gun douse his light. He peered from the window but could see no one. Then the door downstairs slammed open and a stormtrooper rush of boots washed over the floor.

Gun tucked the itinerary into a canvas pocket, then unlocked Geoff's bedroom window and slid it wide. The guest house was a high-ceilinged structure, true to the Hedman sense of the grandiose. Gun grasped a corner of the bed, dragged it six feet to the window's edge, and tied the arms of Geoff's robe around a post. Draped from the window it cut six feet from the fall. Gun lowered himself to robe's length, pushed off the outside wall with his toes like a rappeler, and let go. He rolled ball-to-heel-to-butt on impact, and by the time he reached the river and reeled in his boat, the needles of feeling were beginning to shiver his feet.

Home. One-thirty A.M. He turned on the power on his thirteen-inch color television, jammed the cassette he had found into the VCR, and stood flat-footed in the middle of the living room floor.

The picture clarified.

Mazy was sitting at a table in a dimly-lighted room, her back straight, arms resting confidently on the carved wooden arms of the chair. On her face Gun recognized the defiance he had struggled against for years. Now she was using it on Lyle Hedman, who sat across the table from her, tapping his long fingers on the tabletop. His lips were moving but there was no sound. Gun quickly stepped forward and turned up the volume, but all he got was a noisy fuzz that masked a low mumble. Mazy shook her head, half smiled, and crossed her arms in front of her. Hedman lifted both his hands in a kind of plea. He leaned forward. He seemed to raise his voice, his face jerking with the movement of his lips, and Mazy turned away from him. As Lyle continued to speak, he aimed both his index fingers at her and the arteries stood out on his neck. Mazy rose from her chair.

Out of the shadows at the back of the room a figure appeared, stepped forward. It was Geoff. Lyle spoke again, and Geoff nodded for Mazy to sit down, which she did. Lyle leaned back in his chair and with his joined fingers made a hammock for his chin. Geoff sat down on his father's side of the table. For several more minutes Lyle continued to speak, his eyes on Mazy, his manner easy and confident. Then he stopped and Mazy gave him a decisive shake of the head.

Now Lyle lifted a single finger and his lips formed the word Watch. He raised his chin and adjusted his gaze to the rear of the room. Mazy turned to see what he was looking at. Two men entered the room. One was handcuffed and blindfolded and being led by the other, who wore the same style of green jumpsuit as the guard Gun had taken the .38 away from.

Hedman said something to the man in green, who nodded and backed his prisoner up against the light blue wall. Mazy turned and shook her head at Lyle. Her lips said no. Her face had gone slack and her eyes were wide, bright with unfocused confusion. Gun dropped into a crouch and pressed the palms of his hands against the floor for balance. He watched the screen and saw Lyle nod his head once and Mazy swing around. The man in green raised his pistol and aimed it at the blindfolded prisoner. From what Gun could tell, the weapon was a .45-caliber revolver. It jumped and jumped again. The man in the blindfold stiffened out against the light blue wall, two roses opening on his chest. His head rolled off his neck onto his right shoulder, and the weight of it seemed to settle the matter of which way to fall. He crumpled to the floor. Mazy looked around at Lyle, who shrugged once and licked his lips, then at Geoff, who was hiding behind his own hands. She looked back at the man who had fallen, then up at the light fixture above her head, and finally straight into the camera. Intelligence had fled from her face and left nothing to replace it. No fear, no terror, nothing at all. Gun reached out and touched her, received a small electrical shock from the screen. Lyle stood up. His jaunty posture was not congruent with the scene he had witnessed. He and Geoff ushered Mazy from the room.

As soon as they had gone out, the man in the green jumpsuit looked into the camera and stuck out his tongue. He clapped, then reached down and offered a hand to the dead man on the floor, who accepted it and was pulled to his feet, then freed from his cuffs. The two of them commenced a celebration of their performance, mugging for the camera, laughing, and smearing blood on their faces. Gun remembered Freddy Cheeseman's words: *Now he's got to go all the way.*

Five minutes later, in bed, not feeling tired but aware that he needed sleep, Gun prayed for the courage to make proper use of the destruction rising in his soul.

31

The telephone rang early, blistering Gun's sleep. He rolled from bed and answered the phone in his shorts.

"Gun, it's Carol. Where in God's name have you been?" Carol's voice sounded stretched and wired.

"Carol. I'm glad to hear you." Gun reached for a kitchen chair and sat. "Kind of early, though."

"I've been trying to get you all week. Damn it, Gun, you worry me."

"I'm fine."

"And lucky. You didn't happen to be playing around Lyle Hedman's place last night, did you?"

"Me?"

"God, I knew it. I knew it was you. The two guards you took out said they got jumped by a gang. Sheriff Bakke believed them, I think."

"How do you know about this?" Gun checked the kitchen clock. "It was only about six hours ago."

"I was up early this morning," Carol said. "I'm a journalist."

"Off the record, then, I'd appreciate your silence on this. Did Bakke tell you anything?"

"Yes. He said apparently there were three or four of you, that you hunted through Hedman's lodge and guest house, that you didn't steal a blessed thing, and that all of you escaped into the rushes."

"That's it?"

"That's it. One thing you aren't, Gun, is clutzy. You didn't drop any clues."

"But Bakke has sworn to 'make the pinch,' right?"

"His words exactly. How did you know?"

"Couple of times a year folks around here get broken into. He always says that."

There was a breath of silence on the line before Gun said, "Carol, I might be needing some help with this whole mess before too long. I don't know that for sure, can't even say what kind of help it might be. Can I call you?"

"You know that, Gun."

"I'd like to think you're in this for more than your dislike of Hedman."

"You know that too, Gun," Carol said.

"I'll call you soon," said Gun. "Hedman's taken Mazy out west. Western Canada. And I don't think he plans to bring her back."

"I'm not sure I follow."

"I could be wrong, but I don't think so. The whole Hedman clan is gone, and I think they intend to get rid of Mazy on the trip."

Carol took a sharp breath. "Gun, I know you don't want to hear this, but it's time to get the cops into the picture. If they've taken her out of state, maybe we can get some agency help."

A window patch of reflected sunlight moved across Gun's wall, and his ears picked up the crunch of tires on gravel.

"Where did they take her?" Carol said. "'Western Canada' is a little vague."

"Someone just drove in," said Gun. "I'll call you later."

"Please, Gun. We might not be able to do all this ourselves."

"I'll call you. I promise," said Gun. He tried to hang up tenderly.

An angular blue sedan was sitting in the yard. Gun was startled when the driver slid out and stood, looking uncomfortably around. It was Reverend Barr. He was evidently in no hurry to get to the front door. Gun had time to find his pants.

"Good morning, Gun. I, ah, see you're up." Gun had opened the door just as Barr raised his knuckles to knock.

Barr was clerically dressed in humble brown tweed and a cardboard collar. His shoes were scuffed and apologetic, matching his manner. "Early church starts in another hour or so," he said, his eyes sliding down to his wristwatch. "I thought maybe we could talk."

"Go ahead," said Gun.

Barr's eyes met Gun's for an instant and from there bounced to his chest, forehead, the doorframe, and background behind. They settled at last on a small mole on Gun's cheek, below his right eye. He looked earnestly at the mole. He said, "Gun Pedersen, I'm a man of God. This doesn't come easily for me. I've a confession to make."

Gun crossed his arms.

"You know what my stand has been on this Loon Country thing," Barr said. "No secret, I've been pushing for it. But things have gotten beyond my control. Beyond anyone's. And I think your daughter's in deep trouble."

Gun felt a willful violence rising up inside, a frosty

wish to reach forth and close Barr's windpipe. He said, "Talk fast."

Barr's gaze dropped from the mole to Gun's chest, which was nearer his eye level. His voice withered. "It was Lyle Hedman's idea," he said. "Lyle came to me months ago. Flattered me. He said I had the biggest parish in Stony—that's true—and told me I needed a new church. A big one."

"So?"

Barr reddened over the white collar. "Maybe you don't understand. There are better ways of making money than ministering, especially out here in the sticks. But there aren't many better ways of gaining influence. A big church can mean big power, Pedersen, if you work things right."

"So you sold out to Hedman. Should that surprise me?"

"I don't give a damn if you're surprised," Barr said, forgetting his humility.

"Get to the point. Where's Mazy?" He thought, Say Calgary, Reverend, and we've got a match.

"Everything started turning bad when Rutherford got killed," Barr said. "He was our ace. Old friend of mine from the Cities. Used to come to my church down there."

"Mazy," Gun said.

"Please, let me finish. I need to do this."

"Be quick, Reverend."

Barr lowered his eyes to Gun's knees in theatrical penitence. "Rutherford accomplished his purpose. He helped us bring Tig Larson over to our point of view."

"Poor, brave Tig."

"Then Lyle got worried. Said we were in trouble if Rutherford ever talked. Said we had to be sure that wouldn't happen. He had it done."

"Why are you talking to me? Why aren't you talking to the cops about all this, if you're so damned sorry?"

Again Barr's weak composure split. "Goddamn you, Pedersen, I'm telling you because it's your own kid that's going down next. Unless you can stop it."

Gun's arm snapped out in a backhand rope that knuckled Barr across the temple. The minister reeled on his feet while Gun gripped his stiff collar and pulled him up on his toes. "Confession's over," he said. "Now you tell me where Hedman took her, and tell me right, and tell me fast. Or I'll put you on the other side before you've been forgiven."

"Calgary," Barr slurred. "West of there. Then to British Columbia. Hedman told me the whole family was going, sort of a honeymoon trip in honor of Geoff and Mazy. Only Mazy's not coming back."

Gun lifted Barr two inches off the ground. "She's coming back," he said. "Alive. And healthy." Still holding him by the collar, Gun dragged the minister into the house. Barr sat at the kitchen table with his face in his fingers while Gun fished for an atlas. When he returned and laid it open on the table, a pink, porous knoll had raised on Barr's temple.

It was fairly simple on the map. From Calgary Barr traced a highway across the border into British Columbia, and a winding provincial road into the higher territory of the Canadian Rockies.

"It's the only cabin for a hundred square miles," said Barr. "I pray to God you can find it in time. I wish I had a daughter, Pedersen."

"Lucky for her you don't." Gun picked Barr out of the chair by his collar and skidded him to the door. "Enjoy your last sermon, Reverend. And stay around. I don't want to have to come looking."

"I'll face whatever I have to," Barr said. He managed a sore smile that looked right under his lump. "I'm ready to make amends. As soon as you get back."

32

"He's a shyster in a pulpit, Gun. How much can you afford to believe him?" Jack was speaking forcefully to break through the noise of the truck, which was barreling northward. When they'd departed Sunday evening, it had been a cool day in June, but the nearer they came to the Canadian border, the more May seemed to step back in. Gun rolled up his window, quieting the cab a little.

"Enough to get me to British Columbia," he said. He looked at Jack, who was sitting straight-backed in the Ford for a better view over the high dash. Jack's chin was tough rock, unconvinced. "I keep seeing that look in Mazy's eyes," Gun added. He had shown the tape to Jack before they left.

"Can't blame you for that."

"Don't worry," Gun said. "I know old Barr could've been making it up, trying to get me out of Stony until after the referendum. But I think he was telling the truth. Look at this." Gun pulled the flight itinerary from the pocket of his flannel shirt and shook it open.

It took Jack a moment to decipher the note's significance. He handed it back to Gun, wiped a palm over his black-bristled scalp, and stared forward at the highway. "Five round trips and a one-way," he said. "How'd you get hold of that?"

Gun rolled his shoulders and said nothing, looking straight out over the wheel. He reopened his window an inch and let the wind whistle in. He knew Jack was watching him.

"I heard about half a story on the radio this morning," Jack said. "Early news report. Some gang of vandals on the Hedman place. Didn't steal anything, though."

"Didn't steal *much*," said Gun. "I hear Sheriff Bakke has vowed to make the pinch, though."

"Good to hear," Jack said. "I feel safer, knowing that."

Gun had made the drive from Stony to Winnepeg before. Depending on the time of the year, it took between three and four hours to traverse the northwest quarter of Minnesota, then another ninety minutes from the border across the wavy fields and willowy lowlands of lower Manitoba. He had made the trip once in late December to pick up Mazy on a Christmas flight from San Diego, and the snow beating across the Canadian prairie had nearly frozen him for a holiday funeral. He'd put the old Ford into neutral three, four, five times while getting out to heave at the back bumper. But this was June, backing into May, and he was catching a flight, not meeting one. Gun tapped the dash impatiently with the tips of his wide fingers.

The rattling of the truck and the growing spaces between water towers in Minnesota's extreme northwest made both men thoughtful and anxious. Gun was surprised once to look down and see the needle quivering past the eighty mark. Jack cracked the knuckles of both hands with a noise like the Fourth of July.

"I think she's okay," Gun said. "So far. The round trippers aren't due to come back until Wednesday."

"When this is over, I want Hedman," Jack said.

"I want Mazy first. Then we'll talk about who gets Lyle."

They made the border about eleven at night. A tall, square-shaped guard in a gray uniform stepped out of the concrete customs office. He looked too big to fit back in. Gun rolled down his window.

"Destination," said the guard, shaking his legs one at a time, as if to dispel cramps.

"Winnipeg," said Gun.

"Any alcohol on board?"

"Nope."

"Firearms?"

"Nope."

"Length of stay," said the guard. His feet were planted now, and his palms jammed to his hips. He did a deep back arch, speaking to the sky. "I'm supposed to ask that," he said.

"Forty-eight hours," said Gun. "At the most."

The guard put both hands at the back of his neck and did a round-the-world with his head. "Have a nice night," he said. Gun could hear the stiffness creak in the guard's neck even over the Ford's idle.

"You too," said Gun. He upshifted and nosed the truck toward Winnipeg.

The airport was clean concrete and Sunday-night barren. Gun drove into the parking ramp and took a pink ticket that poked like a tongue from the humming metal box. "Two nights," said Gun. "Twenty bucks Canadian."

"They have such pretty money," said Jack.

The woman at the airline desk smiled at Gun and told him about the delay. "They're experiencing severe thunderstorm conditions over Alberta right now," she said. "Nobody's flying in at all. There's a snack bar down the hall, to pass the time."

"Nobody's flying in? No charters, nothing?" said Gun. He leaned down close to the woman's orchard cheeks.

"We're in contact with the Calgary airport, sir. No takeoffs, no landings." The woman tilted her face up to Gun's. "And that's it, sir, until further notice. There is a snack bar, though, to help pass the time."

Gun straightened and sighed and looked at Jack. He said, "Coffee?"

"It'll pass the time," said Jack.

The snack shop owned a dozen round white tables, anchored to the floor by steel legs, and a self-serve spigot that gave forth clear and ineffectual coffee. Jack inhaled at the rim of his Styrofoam cup. "It doesn't have a smell," he said.

The white-faced clock next to the Snack Shop sign read 9:15. They should have been in the air by now. Gun watched the clouds through the high west windows. It would be three hours by plane, another two or three to gather some necessities and search out Hedman's cabin. The actual work, getting in and getting out, the cleanup job, fifteen minutes tops. About six hours, Gun figured. It had better be enough. He shut his eyes, imagining the storm over Calgary.

They each drank about a dozen cups of coffee before a woman's voice came out of the ceiling with the news that flights to Alberta were getting ready to board. Gun's stride made Jack jog to keep pace as they went to the concourse, through the metal-witching doorframe, down the canvas-topped tube to the 727.

First class meant breathing room for Gun's knees. "Guy could do aerobics in here," said Jack. It was one P.M.

The flight began smoothly, the Boeing lifting itself in a two-hundred-mile wedge to proper elevation, and got lumpy over western Saskatchewan. Calgary's storm front was carrying east.

"We're hitting some turbulence now," intercommed the captain's voice. "Please remain calm and keep your seat belts fastened."

"I'm calm," said Jack. Arms crossed, he looked short and tight as a fifty-gallon drum in the contoured seat. Jack's eyes were at the window, a cloudy-milk square. "Never flown before," he said.

"First-time flyers," said the captain, "think of this as a bumpy road. Lots of potholes."

The 727 hit a deep pothole and Gun felt himself lift briefly from the seat. The belt held him down. He thought, Is this what Amanda felt? The pressure was flat across his hips. He saw Jack's fingers squeeze the armrests. A baby back in coach hiccuped, then howled.

"We're thirty thousand feet above Moose Jaw," said the pilot. "These bad roads should be settling out real soon."

"They buried Jeremy Devitz today," Gun said, trying to see down through the clouds.

"I've been thinking about Bowser."

"Me too."

They landed in Calgary on a blacktop runway slippery with rain. Gun's thick flannel could not seal out the chill, and he realized this trip could have been better planned. It was cool down here in the city, and Hedman's retreat was across the border into a province known mainly for trees and altitude. It would be cooler there. Much cooler.

"You know the way, right?" said Jack.

"About a hundred miles west," said Gun, "and a mile or so straight up."

The dapper young man at the Avis desk quoted them a low, low price for the Jeep they wanted. "Some places would charge you a third more than that," he said, his teeth white as slivered almonds. "And paying that kind of money really Hertz. Heh, heh."

"Thanks," Gun said. He took the keys.

"Idiot," Jack grumbled.

On the west edge of town they located a false-fronted pawn shop with Oriental throwing stars in the windows and a locked rack of guns behind the counter. A woman Gun's age with hair like an orange Lava lamp undid the lock and handed them weapons for inspection.

"What you goin' after?" the woman said. Her voice was Lucille Ball's, a tin scraper. "Moose, out of season. Elk, out of season. Bear, out of season. Hey?"

"Varmints," said Jack. Lucy smiled and turned back to the rack. Her hips hung on her like rucksacks full of birdshot. One of them supported a leather-holstered .357.

"We got plenty of those," she said. "Good luck."

The choice was limited. Gun picked an Ithaca Model 37 twelve-gauge with a Deerslayer barrel, a goose gun modified for slugs. The ammo was heavy and expensive. Jack chose a Savage over-and-under. He bought a box each of twelve-gauge and 30–30 ammunition. "For close-range or far-away varmints," he explained.

Lucy grinned. "Or several varmints at once."

They paid for the guns, leather gloves, and two woolen parkas, black-and-green buffalo plaid. Lucy called to them as they left the shop.

"You two are real cute," she said, waving the bills

they'd stacked on the counter. "Now I never want to hear from you again."

As the Jeep left Calgary and began its ascent, the time-and-temp billboard of a stucco-sided bank showed fifty degrees and three-thirty P.M. "Jack," Gun said, "you got a watch."

Jack read his wrist. "Four-thirty."

Gun remembered. "The time change," he said. "We skipped a zone. We've got another hour." Gun leaned back in the Jeep and stepped on the gas. A spray of weighted raindrops snapped suddenly across the windshield, like hand-flung pebbles.

33

Samuel Barr had fingered a highway leading west out of Calgary some seventy miles before swinging north into spiky pine hills. Gun drove the Jeep at hazardous speeds, but the roads were so bad it was almost three hours before they saw the yellow crossroads sign the minister had described. It had been mistreated with a big-game rifle. "One whole corner of it's been shot away," Barr had said, nursing his lump over Gun's atlas. "You gotta take a right."

Gun took a right onto a road deep with sugar sand. Jack flipped open the Jeep's glove box and pulled out a folded road map. He pressed it flat against his knees. "Gee, this is handy," he said. "Florida. With a detail of Orlando on the back side." He rustled the map back into the glove box. "Gun," he said, "how come Barr knew about that blown-up road sign?"

"Said he'd been out here before. With Hedman. Fishing trip."

"I was thinking," Jack said, "that I really hate being put into the position of having to trust that guy."

"Yup."

"That's the position Rutherford was in."

"Rutherford didn't know the size of the game he'd got into. We do."

The sugar sand subsided as the path led upward, as if the road's entire surface had crumbled loose one rainy night and slipped down the grade to congregate as talus at the bottom. What remained was an adobe-hard trail with craters and black canals that slapped and ground at the four-wheel drive. Gun flipped on the headlights in the thickening dusk. Near the crest of a steep climb a well-tended trail branched right.

"Kenya Drive," said Gun. "Canada style."

The Hedman cabin was nearly a mile through the thick dark pines by foot. The trail would have been easily passable by Jeep, but the engine's loud growl would announce them like a banner on a pole. If it hadn't already. Gun squeezed the Ithaca in his chilled fingers and reminded himself that there were at least five people in that cabin besides Mazy. The surprise would have to be total.

The two of them separated on the walk in, each moving about thirty feet to one side of the trail. The sun was below the rim now. Evergreens shaded to gray. Some distance to his left Gun could catch the occasional glow of Jack's Savage. The pine needles were quiet as corn silk under Gun's boots and sent up the smell of fresh creation.

Another smell gave them their first alert. A slow evening wind reached across Gun's face and brought with it a swish of sweet tobacco. He stopped. Jack was standing stone-silent. Gun's twilight vision picked out the blued Savage barrel, pulled to a ready forty-five degrees. Neither one moved. The tobacco smell increased with the wind, then faded. They held position for a thick quarter hour and eyed the trees, which grew lighter the higher they looked. Straight overhead Gun could see their tops still getting touched by sun. The smell arrived again on the breeze, and following its direction back with his eyes, Gun saw the source.

A man in a dark spruce Army jacket perched on a stool in a tree stand at the head of the trail. The stand was about nine feet high and constructed of two-by-fours, which had gone gray with weather—a deer stand, Gun thought. Deer were out of season.

It was still light enough to catch Jack's eye. Jack nodded and the stalk began again, slower now. The man in the stand was holding an open-sighted rifle across his knees. His head was helmeted in a bush of rabbit fur. Puffs of smoke floated up from his face and were curled off on the wind. As they came nearer, Gun and Jack began to converge, vee-ing in on the tree. Gun was grateful for the man's rabbit cap. It must have blocked a measure of sound.

They reached the foot of the tree just as the moon peeked up over the hills behind the cabin. The guard looked up at it and shifted his butt on the little stool. Gun reached high and gripped a two-by-four support.

The stand came down with less effort than Gun had expected. The guard gave forth only the noise of an amazed inhale before Jack knelt and put his compact strength into a cheekbone punch.

"He sleeps," Jack said, standing. He shook his hand, fingers splayed. "Ow."

"For how long?"

"Two, three hours," said Jack. His Roman face produced a short grin. "All that sneaking around kind of wound up my spring."

They emptied the guard's 30-06 and tossed the shells into the trees. The cabin was a Hedman-sized structure of stripped logs standing off across a wild-flower clearing. A yellow yardlight burned next to a square-stacked woodpile. Someone had started a fire, and the smell of smoke and coffee lifted from the chimney.

"We'd better stay back," Gun said. "Far enough in so we can't be seen from the yard. We'll take the cabin from the rear."

"They might have another guard up somewhere."

"Maybe. I don't think they'd stick two guys up in trees."

The low-profile hike kept the cabin in constant view and took another thirty minutes. The moon was an indistinct platter behind the haze when they reached a set of red pines twenty yards off the back porch.

"Let's go in like wild men," Jack said softly. His cheeks were ruddy as a child's, and Gun thought he could feel a schoolground heat come off him. "Butch and Sundance," Jack whispered. He was crouching, as wide in that position as he was tall.

"You go around to the front door," said Gun. "I'll get up on the back porch. We'll meet in the middle."

"See you in about five minutes," Jack said, and he went, the Savage looking mean but comfortable riding in his hand. He reached the left rear corner of the cabin, paused there, threw a grin back at the trees. It made Gun wonder at their bravado. Three, four rifles at least inside that cabin, and he and Jack outside, talking like third graders about cutting down enemy cornstalks. Butch and Sundance.

Now Jack was gone from sight, rolling up the left side of the cabin, no doubt moving fast to reach the door. Gun stooped only slightly—if anyone were looking, six-and-a-half feet would be seen whether he was bent over or not—and made the porch. Like everything else Hedman owned, the cabin was well-built. The porch boards didn't creak under Gun's weight. He crept to a window, tilted a glance inside, saw three heavy men at a knotty-pine table. They wore buttoned underwear shirts and black suspenders. Real lumberjacks. They were eating ham steaks. Gun wondered where Lyle was, wondered if Lyle was even along, and then he heard the door.

It slammed at the front of the cabin, and at first Gun thought Jack had gone in. But there was no noise afterward. Gun moved across the window and stood next to the porch door, his back against log siding. If anyone had come out, he hadn't seen Jack. There was no disturbance. Gun gripped the door handle and set himself. He pulled the Ithaca ready. He was taken by surprise when someone tall, not Jack, appeared in his corner vision.

"Hey!" the guard yelled. He was evidently surprised too, but recovered quickly enough to unholster the .44 at his hip.

"Drop it," Gun said. The Ithaca was aimed. The tall man did not register the action. He fired the pistol, and Gun felt hot teeth tear at the flesh of his left ribs. He stayed steady and shot the guard through the chest.

Gun's shirt and jacket were drawing blood, and now the air was soaked with noise. Dark roars as the lumberjacks seized their guns, the steely snap of a rifle from the front of the cabin, yells crowding each other for help. Gun's ears pulled Mazy's voice from the mob. He pumped a new slug into the chamber and put his shoulder to the door.

The lock broke on the second blow and Gun swung in off balance. A white-faced guard, braced before a door on the right-hand wall, took hurried aim and released a buckshot charge. The Ithaca snaked in Gun's hand and came up with the stock blown off. Gun flung the barrel at the guard and dove for the nearest cover, a wide woodstove that stood out from the wall. The guard's shotgun blasted again but the stove was stern iron and sent buckshot rocketing. The stove still held fire, and Gun was grateful for his thick woolen coat and gloves. Through the hell of shotgun roar and lead fire Gun could feel the heavy shake of cabin walls, as though a bear were belting the logs. He heard a wild barking laugh outside. He heard, from somewhere behind the panicked guard, a willful angry scream from Mazy. The scream tore at a nerve of memory and pain, and Gun stood without thinking and gripped the stove in his leathered hands.

The guard howled as Gun raised the stove from the floor. Rivets made peeling metal shrieks as the chimney flue came in two. An elbowed section of twelve-inch pipe hung on the wall, dropping cinders. Gun staggered forward, the stove out front. The guard fired once more before Gun reached him, and this time several pellets entered Gun's vulnerable legs. The stove became impossibly heavy. His hands and chest smoked against the black iron. He felt himself come near the guard, and the guard's howl come from ahead and meet behind him, and then the stove came down. Gun's nostrils jerked at a cannibal heat. His hands were scorched like the lids of cutout pumpkins. The guard was silent beneath the woodstove, which sat angled on its side and coughed up ashes through its broken spout.

"Who's out there?" quailed a voice. It came from behind the door where the guard had stood. Gun recognized it.

"Just me, Geoff," he said. "Now get my girl out here. Before this place burns." Live sparks were spattering from the stove. One flamed up in the sleeve of the guard. Gun stamped it out.

"Dad?" The lock clacked, the door inched open. Gun heard Mazy's voice, but Geoff's face filled the crack.

"She's okay, Mr. Pedersen," said Geoff.

Gun didn't answer. He pushed through Geoff and saw Mazy sitting on an ill-made bed.

"Dad. You're hurt."

They heard the front door slam and Jack coughing as he went past the smoldering stove. "Gettysburg," he said, beating the air before his face. "Mazy! You're okay?" He caught sight of Geoff, on his butt in shock, and looked at him as though considering a kick to the crotch.

Geoff spoke slowly from the floor, head in his hands. "You guys are nuts."

"Shut up, Geoff," said Gun, looking hard at Mazy. "You aren't here at all."

34

"Did they hurt you?" Gun said, on his back. Mazy was dabbing at his ragged side with a cloth, which made him pinch his words.

"I'm all right. Believe me." She kept her eyes on the wound. "This is ugly. What did he shoot you with, a cannon?"

"A .44, and I'm glad he was in a hurry," said Gun. Jack had doused the gutted stove and opened windows to clear the smoke. Gun was on the bed.

"I didn't have any choice, Dad. I hated all the lying. They had me, was all." Mazy gripped Gun's wrist for a moment, suspending the rag above the ripped skin. "But you knew that. You could tell." Gun reached up and ran a finger along Mazy's cheekbone. She stopped it with her hand. "Couldn't you?" she asked.

"You could've been less convincing."

Mazy wiped hair from her forehead with the back of her hand. "It must have been rough on Barr's ego, coming to you and spilling it like that. All part of the production, just to get you out here."

"What about the rest of it? You and Geoff."

Mazy shrugged, a slim-shouldered gesture like her mother's. "Marriage *papers* are real enough. But there's no marriage. No baby, either." Her face went from relief to anger. "Won't Lyle's family doctor be surprised."

"Will be, when he gets back from the Riviera. Where's Hedman?"

"Might be anywhere. He drove out of Stony behind Geoff and I. Annison drove separately. Always does."

"Annison?"

"Lyle's wife," Mazy said, pausing for a glance at Geoff, whose face was dark. "Geoff's mother."

"Sounds like a headache pill," said Jack. He ragged his hands free of ash on a corner of bedspread. "We had it figured, about the setup."

"You came, though," Mazy said. Gun glared at Geoff, who was sitting up straight now, his arrogance returning.

Mazy rinsed the cloth in a basin. When Gun's side and legs were clean and wrapped in layers of cotton, the four of them walked away from the cabin toward the road.

The Jeep pulled into the Calgary airport at eleven P.M., midnight in Stony. Gun booked four one-ways on American to Winnipeg. Then he went to a pay phone on the wall next to the flight desk. He reached Carol at the newspaper office on the ninth ring.

"Where in heaven or hell are you calling from!" she blew. "No. Don't tell me. I think I know."

"What did you expect?" Gun said.

"Damn it, Gun, you like doing this!"

"Mazy's all right. So is Jack. So am I."

"You're more than all right," Carol said. "You sound like a kid who's been out playing cavalry."

"I guess we have been," Gun said calmly. He told her about Barr's confession, about the sudden flight, about the cabin in the woods with Mazy inside it. He didn't mention the small war and its casualties.

"If Barr told you all that just to set you up, then how did you get out of there? And with Mazy?"

Gun shut his eyes, inhaled.

"You fought them, didn't you? Did you get hurt? Did anybody get hurt?"

"Carol, three of them are dead. None of them were Hedman."

"My God." Gun imagined Carol biting her emerald ring.

"I need your help now. All of us do."

"What can I do?"

"Is it possible to put out a special edition of the *Journal*? Can you fire up the presses a little early?"

"I can if I need to. I'll have to do it without my regular help."

"It's important, Carol." Gun gripped the phone too hard, and his palm, red as fire, opened without permission. He caught the receiver with a forearm against his chest and juggled it back to his ear. "We have two witnesses now, Geoff Hedman and Barr. First you've got to secure Barr. Get him out of commission."

"Out of commission."

"Lure him in, knock him out, lock him up. Somewhere. Keep him cold until we get back. We're going to need him."

"I'll try." Carol sounded winded. "What about the paper?"

"I want you to write an article. News, editorial, call it what you like. People read your paper. Tell them how their good reverend got his buddy Rutherford to set up Tig Larson, and then let him go down under Hedman."

"Hold it, Gun." Carol was scribbling audibly. "If I do this, if I print this, all of it had better come out. In court. If one fragment of this isn't proven, I'm throwing twenty years of news work out a high window."

"It'll stick," Gun said. "If you're afraid, don't write the article and we'll get through it another way. But Lord, Carol, it might make the difference."

"Difference in what? You've got a witness with you. Bring him home."

"The difference might be whether Hedman goes to jail, or I do. And Jack. We just left a few of Hedman's pals out in the woods, but he has a lot more. In strategic positions, I'd bet."

Carol bit her ring. Gun could see it.

"If you write it," he said, "include everything. Don't leave anything out. Only the unabridged version will do."

Carol's voice was dark and sharp, obsidian. "When will you get back?"

"Tomorrow afternoon. We're flying to Winnipeg on American. We'll drive from there."

"Drive fast," Carol said.

35

The DC-10 touched down in Winnipeg at one-thirty. The sun was starting to burn a hole through heavy skies, a silver drizzle was angling down before a clearing west wind, and Carol Long was waiting at the airport. She was the first person Gun saw as he and Mazy stepped from the debarking tunnel. He was surprised at the rush of joy he felt at seeing her. She wore a bright red sweatshirt. Her hair looked coal black. Her face was drawn and pale. She swept past Gun and threw her arms around Mazy. Then she pulled away and touched Mazy's chin with the fingertips of both hands.

"And you came through it fine," Carol said. "Thank God." Her eyes were dry and steady, but there was a slight tremor in her chin.

Jack came down out of the tunnel flattening back his greasy crew cut with both hands. He smiled at Gun, then at the women. Geoff stood looking at his feet.

Gun said to Carol's back, "How'd it go last night?"

"Just fine," she snapped, turning. "I did everything exactly as requested." Her glare was brief and freezing.

They stopped at a gun shop to replace the dead Ithaca, then headed south for Minnesota. Gun and Mazy rode in Carol's car, Jack followed with Geoff in Gun's pickup. By three-thirty they'd been on the road half an hour and Mazy was curled sleeping in the backseat. Gun was driving, holding the wheel as lightly as he could because of the burn blisters on his hands. He sipped at a giant Styrofoam cup of coffee he'd picked up at the airport. The coffee was cool but jumping with caffeine. He could feel it in the back of his head, a soft, pulsating pain, and though his body was exhausted, his eyes felt like mechanical shutters stuck wide open.

Carol was silent and staring out the passenger window at the long, greenish-brown reach of Manitoba prairie. So far Gun had honored her apparent wish to be left alone, but now he decided her silence seemed self-indulgent. He cleared his throat.

"So you don't feel like talking," he said.

She ignored him.

"And it's because I left without telling you what was up."

Carol leaned toward him. "Your daughter's trying to sleep," she said.

Gun looked sideways at her, rubbing the unburned heel of his right hand against his two-day stubble. He said, "Do you think I would have done what I did if I thought there was a better way?"

Carol looked at him, and their eyes met for an instant before she turned away. "Probably not. But I don't think that says much for your judgment." She brought up her feet and curled herself into the seat, facing the passenger door.

"Fair enough," Gun said.

The sky had cleared as much as it was going to for a while. The drizzle had stopped, but the sun was still nothing more than a dull yellow beach ball in the gray sky. Gun could tell by the arch in Carol's shoulders that she wasn't anywhere near falling asleep, and her left hand, resting on her leg, was a hard white fist. He said, "Carol, maybe you ought to tell me what happened last night. This isn't over yet."

"I suppose I'd better," she muttered into the window. She twisted around in her seat, pulled herself upright. "I wrote the article, took it to the printer, and locked up Barr in a safe place." She spoke quickly, then clamped her mouth shut.

Gun blinked. "You actually locked him up," he said. He saw Carol start to smile.

"He's in your new boathouse," she said.

He smiled and swung into the passing lane to overtake a truck pulling a hay rack loaded with scrap iron. He laughed, trying to picture it: Barr in his stiff black-and-white collar and his carefully pressed pants, sitting there in the dark on the dirt floor, or maybe in the old Alumacraft, on one of the life cushions. He was probably getting some good practice in sincere prayer. "How'd you get him in there, anyway?"

"I had good help." Now Carol smiled in spite of herself. "My son showed up last night, at supper-time."

"No kidding. From California."

"He wanted to see the 'rugged north country.'"

"Turned out to be more rugged than he expected, I bet."

"I'd say so, yes." Carol's voice had lost its tightness, sounded natural again. "Mike and I drove over to Barr's house. No one was home, so we tried the church. There was a light in his office. I left Mike in the car, and he covered up with a few blankets and coats in the backseat while I went to Barr's door and knocked. When he saw me he lit up like a Christmas tree. You know his capacity to gloat—here it was the night before the referendum, victory just hours away, the new cathedral probably cementing itself together in his fantasies—he was thrilled to see me. Asked me in for coffee. I told him thanks, but we had something to discuss. Someone had leveled serious charges against him, and I wanted to hear his side of the story before I wrote it up." Carol paused, gave Gun a self-satisfied smile. "Believe me, I was winging it. Had no idea what I was going to tell him. I just wanted to get him out to the car. Finally I said that one of Hedman's people, the cook, had phoned me up with a story about bribes and collusion. The reverend sobered up in a hurry. I said I'd arranged to meet the cook at my place, and would he like to come along. So off we went."

Gun swallowed the last of his cold coffee and grinned into the cup.

"Then we took Barr out to your boathouse. I think Mike's still in shock. His mom, the conspirator."

"How'd you get the boathouse open? I had it padlocked, I think."

"Before Mike and I went over to Barr's, we stopped at old man Calvert's, borrowed his lock clipper and bought a new one."

"So Barr's just waiting for us, then."

"He's waiting, all right. The question is how we're going to reach him." Carol sighed, then looked at Gun hard, her pupils bright as knife points. "This is the part I haven't told you yet. Hedman's got roadblocks on every road leading into the county."

Gun could almost feel his brain notch into gear and start spinning off possibilities.

Carol said, "My paper hit the stands at eight-thirty this morning, and you'd better believe it caused a stir.

Hedman called me at a quarter to nine, just before I left. He threatened to have me arrested."

"For what?"

"He wasn't too specific."

"Tell me about the roadblocks."

"Like I said, every road leading into the county. Highways, township roads, everything. Tar and gravel. The official version is that 'suspected felons' are in the area; Sheriff Bakke loves his sweet ambiguities. But Hedman's had every one of his paper-mill workers deputized. He's taking no chances."

"I'm flattered," Gun said.

They drove on under overcast skies, crossed through customs without incident and continued southeast, the low marshland of the northern counties stretching out on both sides of the road, the real pine country still a hundred miles off. Half an hour beyond the border, Gun pointed at a green sign that said, HOPE, 5 MILES. "There's a good little café there," he said. "Anybody hungry?"

"I am," said Mazy from the backseat. She sat up and leaned forward, pushing her face between the bucket seats. "You two look nice together," she said.

36

Gun parked in front of a small brick café on a mostly boarded-up Main Street. The sign painted in red letters across the big picture window said FAT FREDDIE's. In smaller letters below, it said *Post Office in Rear: Hope, Minnesota 56362.*

"You sure about this?" Carol asked.

"Freddie eats his own cooking," Gun answered.

They got out of the Horizon and stretched. Jack and Geoff came rumbling up in Gun's pickup. Gun walked to Jack's window.

"Geoff behaving himself?"

Geoff leaned forward. His face had gotten older on the drive. "You guys are done," he said. "All done. You might as well let me off here."

"Surly child," said Jack.

They were given the window booth. The place wasn't particularly clean, but the burgers were thick, the buns homemade. Fat Freddie was nowhere to be seen. Gun ate quickly and finished first, then gave a summary of Carol's news from Stony. As he spoke he took out a small pearl-handled jackknife and started working on his fingernails. "Hedman might have all the roads into the county sealed off," he said. "But there's another way in. By water. The northern tip of Stony Lake juts over the county line. All we need to do is reach the lake, find a boat, and head for my place. We pick up Barr and motor on into town, right up to the docks at the Muskie Lounge. If the referendum's passed, and you can bet it will have, the celebration will be in full swing."

"Where's the boat going to come from?" Carol asked.

"There are lots of good boats up there on the north end. We'll get a friend to lend us one."

"It might not be so easy for you to find a friend tonight," Carol said.

"Maybe not," Gun agreed. "But when I need to, I can turn on the charm." He pointed his jackknife at her.

"I think tonight you'll need to."

"You watch," Gun said.

The waitress came with the check and set it down in front of Jack, who slid it over to Gun. "You're treating, right?"

The waitress now at the till was older, with red eyes and orange lipstick. Her cheeks were broad, the skin starting to sag. "Your face," she said, waving the twenty Gun handed her. "I could swear I've seen it."

"I don't think so," Gun said.

They left Fat Freddie's. Gun was following Geoff down the sidewalk when suddenly Geoff turned. "Gun," he said. "I really need some cigarettes. Mind if I run back in?"

"Didn't know you smoked."

"Only when I'm nervous."

"I'll go in with you." Gun steered Geoff back inside by an elbow.

Geoff told the woman at the till he wanted three packs of Camels, then picked up a pen from the counter and started writing a check. Gun stopped him and paid for the cigarettes with a five.

"My treat. Let's get going." He took Geoff's elbow, but Geoff pulled away.

"I should use the can. Before we take off." Geoff's face verified the urgency in his voice.

Gun waited outside the men's room. "Feel better?" he said when Geoff emerged. Geoff only smiled and shrugged his shoulders.

Back on the road the barren lowlands began to give way to an occasional hill populated with scrub pines. The wind seemed to be coming from the west and south at the same time, and Gun suspected about sundown it would switch around to the east again. The thinning cloud cover would firm up and drop down low, making good darkness.

Mazy was in the front seat now, Carol in back. It was the first time Gun and his daughter had been alone together since the rescue, and they talked quietly while Carol slept, told each other old family stories. The memories were fresh tonight, pleasant to dwell on, not painful, Gun realized.

"I'm sorry I missed so much," he said.

"It's okay." Mazy leaned back on the headrest and smiled at the ceiling. "Mom said something once, late in the summer. You were on a road trip."

"As usual."

"She told me that missing someone you love is a privilege."

"She was right," Gun said.

Silence. He looked at his daughter, who smiled thinly, turned away. She said, "Sometimes I wasn't sure if you missed her at all. I was afraid the only thing hurting you was the guilt. I wanted to think it was love too."

"Both," said Gun. "A lot of both, Mazy."

"I believe that now. I do."

Gun nodded. He swallowed hard, trying to relax the swelling in his throat. He was afraid to let himself speak again.

37

Gun slowed the car as it neared the crest of a long climb, dark trees rising up on both sides, headlights spearing the low gray clouds like a pair of giant white fingers. Then the road flattened out and Gun pulled onto the gravel shoulder. On a clear night the view from here would be magnificent, an endless reach of black forest, dotted here and there with lights and cleft in two by the liquid expanse of Stony Lake. But the wind had shifted around to the east, as Gun had expected, and tonight not a single light was visible. He shut off the engine and rolled down his window. As if wakened by the silence, Mazy sat up from sleep. No one spoke. Gun could smell the lake. He could feel the cool late-inning buoyancy in the space beneath his heart.

The rumble of the pickup approached from behind. Headlights illuminated the inside of the Horizon, and Gun got out and walked the ten yards back along the gravel shoulder to talk with Jack.

"Let's park in Landsom's gravel pit," Gun said. "We can walk from there, through the federal land."

"You got any ideas about a boat?"

"Yup."

"Let's go, then."

Gun led the way. He continued half a mile on the county road, then took a right and went a quarter mile on township gravel. Just past an empty farmhouse he turned right again, then followed a curving, rutted drive that cut through heavy woods. The gravel pit was about a hundred yards in, an old dig no longer used and overgrown with weeds. It looked like a moon crater. At the far end was Landsom's rusty combine, sitting there as it had for years, like a frozen dinosaur.

"We'll walk in from here," Gun said. He parked behind the combine. "It's only a quarter mile to the lake. Straight that way." He pointed into the woods, due south.

Jack pulled up alongside in the pickup. Gun walked back to the trunk of the Horizon, opened it, brought up artillery. The Savage over-and-under, a Remington 870 twelve-gauge he'd picked up in Winnipeg, boxes of shells.

"You said this was going to be easy," Carol said, slamming the door of the Horizon and striding toward Gun. "Get a boat, pick up Barr, cruise into town. Nothing to it."

"That's right."

"So what are those for?" She pointed at the shotguns.

Gun didn't answer. Jack leaned into the bed of the pickup and held up a long fish-cleaning knife in a leather sheath. "For you, Carol. Just in case." He reached over and slid the blond-handled knife into the front pocket of her jeans.

218

Carol stroked the knife's handle and frowned. "What kind of trouble are you guys expecting?" she said, a ripple in her voice.

"Maybe none," Gun said.

"Maybe more of what we had out west," Jack added.

Carol's eyes were on the shotguns and troubled. She said, "I'm afraid having weapons along will only make things worse. Gun"—she drew the fish-cleaning knife from the sheath in her pocket, its blade long and slightly curved—"I'm starting to think you really *want* this. A physical confrontation. You and Lyle . . . and the law of the jungle." She shot Gun a sarcastic smile.

Gun handed the Savage across to Jack.

Carol said, "Mazy, can't you see what's going on here?"

Mazy shook her head. "I don't think you know what kind of people we're dealing with."

"The kind of people we're dealing with? We're dealing with a bunch of hired deputies, and none of them are the least bit interested in doing us any harm." Carol ignored a chuckle from Jack.

"That's right," said Geoff. Everyone looked at him. He kept his face on the level and his shoulders high, but took a step backward.

Jack said, "Geoff's the only one agreeing with you, Carol."

"You've all got an inflated idea of Lyle Hedman's power," Carol said. Her eyes were bright and her face shone with anger. No one answered.

Gun slid the pump action of his Remington back and forth twice to be sure it wasn't jammed, then thumbed four shells into the magazine, pumped one into the chamber, filled out the magazine with number five, and checked the safe. He looked around the circle of faces. "Time to see about that boat," he said.

Jack loaded his shotgun and they started off, Gun out front, Geoff sandwiched in mid-file, Jack in the rear. The forest was old and relatively free of undergrowth, and in ten minutes they could see Old Stony Road. The lake was twenty yards beyond it, hidden now by a fog rising off the water.

"You all know Lou Young's place, right? It's his boat I'm thinking of. Old Glastron, built like a tank, big Merc on the back. He keeps it on the lift. If I know Lou, it'll be unlocked." Gun glanced around at each face. Jack's chin and cheekbones looked hard as cement. His eyes twinkled like spots of polished granite. Geoff seemed thoughtful, almost confident, gazing off in the direction of the lake. Carol's eyes were dark slants. Half her mouth was turned up in a skeptic's grin. Mazy's face was placid and beautiful, but Gun knew if he touched her arm he'd be surprised at her hardness. As a small girl she'd smiled dreamily through all her shots, yet more than one doctor had broken off needles in her tough little muscles.

"Okay," Gun said. "Let's stay well back from the road until we're opposite the grove of maples that borders east of Lou's property. Then we cross over the road and walk the center of the grove to the lake. From there it's only forty yards or so to the boat. The bank is pretty steep. We stay low and Lou needn't see us."

"I thought your charm was getting us the boat," Carol said.

"Your point." Gun smiled. He motioned with his head and started walking. Across the road from the maple grove they gathered in the darkness below the spreading limbs of an oak. Two sets of headlights passed by. One was a county sheriff's car, headed toward Stony.

220

"He's out of his jurisdiction," Jack said.

"Should've flagged him down, told him so."

Dark again, they crossed the road, stayed to the middle of the grove and made the lake. The water was sheltered from the wind here, and the surface shone with a dark luster, like well-used pewter. To the right, barely visible in the fog, was a small boathouse. Young's heavy runabout hung in front of it, suspended just above the water in the square metal skeleton of the lift.

In a low crouch Gun started toward the boathouse, Carol and the others following. At the near corner of it Gun was stopped by a soft, low growl. He reached back and put a steadying hand on Carol's arm, strained ahead to see some form or concentration of darkness. There was nothing. A dog? Lou had never owned one, Gun was sure of it. Scavenging coon, maybe. Or mink. He'd heard one growl like that once, a thirty-five-inch buck, its foot in a trap. Gun took a slow step forward and his boot snapped a twig. Then a throaty roar exploded in the air, and a shadow of liquid motion leapt from the opposite corner of the boathouse, eyes glowing yellow, body cutting the night like wind. Gun braced himself and brought up his shotgun like a staff. The yellow eyes flew at Gun's neck. Something snapped. There was a hard thump, a choking sound. A floodlight kicked in, washing the lakefront white. A German shepherd lay at Gun's feet, coughing, back legs splayed, front legs pawing at the chain around its neck.

"The hell's going on here!"

Lou Young's lanky figure stood on the sloping ground between his cabin and the boathouse. Gun started up the hill toward him, alone.

"That you, Gun?"

"Sure is, Lou." Gun walked up to him. White curls stuck out from under Lou Young's camouflage hunting cap. He was sucking on a short fat cigar. His old face was nothing but bone and shadow.

"Didn't know you had a dog, Lou," Gun said. He set the stock of his Remington on the grass.

"Don't have a dog," Lou said. "My sister's. She's off for Arizona these two weeks." Lou tilted his head and shot a stream of smoke straight up. "Got a nasty voice, though, don't he?"

Gun nodded. "You're not in town for the doings, Lou."

"Nope." He squinted at Gun. "But I guess you're on *your* way."

"Yup."

"And you want my boat."

"That's right."

"Hedman's got some money on your head, Gun. Not exactly official, but folks know about it. Five grand to whoever gets you on a leash." Lou took the cigar from his lips, hawked, and spit.

"What do you think about that, Lou?"

"I think the man who'd take it is as shit-slimy as the one who's offerin'." Lou looked from Gun down to the lakeshore and nodded toward the boat. "There's a fresh tank of gas. Choke her down halfway till she's warm."

"Appreciate it," Gun said. He turned to leave.

"There's lots of folk like me around," Lou said. "Don't say a whole hell of a lot. Tend to stay out of things, like you do most of the time. But they can't jerk our heads around too easy, neither."

Without turning, Gun lifted a hand in reply and walked on down to the lake. "Lou says we can have the boat," he said.

"Charming," said Carol.

They boarded and motored off into the foggy darkness, the German shepherd setting up a high, mournful howling that pierced the heavy drone of the big outboard. It was a ten-mile trip by water to Gun's place, half an hour. Jack drove. Gun sat close to the starboard gunwale and let his burned hands slice through the cool water. Off Crow Point half a dozen boats worked the walleye hole, but aside from that they were alone on the lake, or seemed to be. Visibility was poor. No moon, no stars. Just the ragged fog that hung in wispy shreds above the water and swept through their faces like clouds through an airplane. The wind had stalled out and the ride was smooth, the boat's headlight beam steady.

They reached Gun's dock at ten-thirty, according to Jack's gold watch with green glow-in-the-dark hands. Mazy tied up the boat.

"Got the jail keys?" Gun said to Carol.

"Sure." She held up a ring.

They walked to the boathouse and gathered in a semicircle at the door. Jack said, "You hungry in there, Reverend?" Carol put the key in the padlock. It didn't snap open. She tried again, shook it. Nothing happened.

"You sure it's the right key?" Gun asked.

"Positive."

"Here. Let me try." Gun leaned the Remington against the wall next to the door, inserted the key and yanked. The lock held. "You all right in there, Barr?" he yelled.

"Fine," came the muffled response.

Jack produced a small flashlight from his pants and looked through Carol's key ring. Gun walked to the woodpile next to his house and came back with a wedge-shaped splitting maul.

"This is ludicrous, it worked before," Carol said.

"Give me a little room," Gun said. He hefted the maul, swung it high, brought it down.

The lock broke under a single swing. Gun pulled the door open and stepped forward with Jack. It was black inside, and suddenly from the blackness sprang a heavy growl and the sharp snap of shell entering chamber. "Damn," whispered Gun.

Another voice said, "Lay it down, LaSalle."

38

Jack bent down slowly and laid the shotgun on the ground. Lyle Hedman stepped out from the shadows of the boathouse with a shotgun of his own, Reuben at his side. Three other men stepped forward and flanked Hedman, one on his right, two on his left. On the right was Horseley, one of the import guzzlers from two nights ago. Tonight he had a .45. Unholstered. The other two men were unfamiliar to Gun. One was close to seven feet tall and big enough to serve as a winter sliding hill for children. He carried a shotgun too, and set a Coleman lantern on the ground. The third man wore long oily black hair, dark glasses, and held a 30-30 at the waist. It was aimed at Gun's midsection.

Hedman pointed at Gun's Remington, which still leaned against the boathouse wall. "Berg, get rid of that," he said. The big man, breathing heavily, took two slow steps backward, picked up the shotgun, and

225

broke it in half against the corner of the stone building.

"The maul, Pedersen," Lyle said.

Gun dropped the splitting maul on the ground. Reuben growled.

Hedman touched the dog's head. "Sorry, boy, you can't have him," he said, then turned and peered into the darkness. "Reverend? It's safe now." Almost immediately, Barr's lean face appeared over Hedman's shoulder.

"Old Samuel's a little nervous," said Lyle. He grinned broadly. "So. Surprised?"

"How did you know?" Carol said.

Geoff laughed and pushed his way between Jack and Mazy to stand at his father's side.

"Good work, Geoff," Lyle said. "It makes things a helluva lot neater."

"Simple job," Geoff said. He turned to Gun, winked. "I got a pen from that cashier, the one in Hope. Wrote a note in the john on toilet paper. I put it on the toilet seat, right there where the next guy would see it. And it worked, damnit! I got the pen pretending I wanted cigarettes—"

"Smart of you, Geoff," Lyle cut in. "Now shut the hell up." Lyle's voice was trembling and the grin was gone from his face. "Gun, Jack, you guys made some hamburger out there in B.C. Congratulations. Hope the war games were fun." He poked Gun in the chest with the barrel of the twelve-gauge. "You're a brave man, aren't you, Pedersen? You and your goddamn big reputation. Hero. Sportsman. Lone wolf. Bullshit. Let me tell you how the public's gonna judge you from now on. They'll hear the name Gun Pedersen and they won't think Detroit Tigers. They'll think killer. And they'll be right. First degree, three counts. I guarantee it. I've got friends, and I've got witnesses. Jerry Drake, for one. He's the guy out there you didn't hit hard enough. Crawled off into the woods with just an egg on his head. Lucky guy. And there's Geoff, he was there. Barr, too, if I wanted to use him to testify, which I don't think will be necessary. Remember the little conversation you and the reverend had before you flew off to Canada? Sunday morning, wasn't it, right out here at your place? You told Barr just what you were planning to do. Told him you were going to kill me and Geoff and anyone else who stood between you and your daughter. You were in a frenzy, remember? Foaming at the mouth. Screaming for revenge. You were going goddamn nuts." Hedman looked over his shoulder at Barr. "Isn't that right, Reverend?"

Barr nodded, sober.

Gun said, "I guess we'll wait. See who the people believe."

Hedman shook his head and gripped one hand around the back of his neck, as if trying to work out a kink. "Shit," he said, "the people are only going to hear one story. That'll make it an easy choice for 'em."

It was silent for a few seconds, then Hedman laughed quietly. "If you think I'm gonna let even one of you say one word to anyone about anything, you must think I'm some kind of idiot." He leaned down and patted Reuben on the head. "Gun, all I can say is it's too bad you had to bring your friends into it. Because you've buried them. Simple as that. Yourself too."

Carol said, "People have already heard the truth, Lyle. They've been reading my paper all day. We turn up dead tomorrow and you won't be far behind."

"Partially right, Carol, partially right. If they found you out here on Gun's beach with bullets in your heads, people might get a little suspicious. But that's not gonna happen. Oh, no. What we're going to have here is a boating accident, plain and simple. You're on your way across the lake at night, sneaking into the county past the roadblocks, guilty as hell. Something happens and your boat goes down. It's a foggy night, see, you're going fast, running careless, and down under Holliman's Bluff you run smack into Crazy Boy Rock." Hedman shifted the weight of his shotgun into the crook of an elbow and slapped his hands together. "And that's it," he said. "Don't forget what happened to young Jimmy Latchfield and his wife. Nasty bruises on their heads, but what do you expect, skull hitting rock at thirty miles an hour. They drowned twenty feet from the rock, and their boat didn't even sink." Hedman draped an arm around Geoff. "Of course, this guy'll survive to tell the story."

"Question for you," said Jack. "If we're as guilty as you say, then what the hell are we doing back here? How does Geoff explain that?"

Hedman licked his lips, tasted each detail. "Geoff tells people that before Gun lit out for British Columbia he had a little conversation with the Reverend Barr, told the man exactly what he was up to. Barr's testimony, in such a case, would be vital. An impartial third-party witness, an influential man of the cloth who can verify that Gun and Jack set out with intent to commit murder. So . . ." Hedman stepped backward and threw a skinny arm about Barr's shoulders, hugged the grinning reverend close. "So here's the deal. Geoff tells everybody that Gun and crew stole across the lake tonight for the express purpose of getting rid of the man who could fill their story with holes. They shot poor Samuel Barr in the heart and then headed back north again, only to barrel into Crazy Boy Rock and drown."

Gun said, "Cheeseman was right. You don't know when it's over."

"Lyle?" Reverend Barr pulled away from Hedman. His smile was frozen horror.

"There's way too much riding on your ability to keep your nerve, Reverend, and I don't think you can," Lyle said.

"But we've been together on this all the way. You know you can trust me. My God!"

Hedman said, "Fraser, hand me LaSalle's shotgun."

The man with the hair and dark glasses did as he was told. Lyle handed his own gun to the big man, Berg. He broke open Jack's over-and-under, made sure it was loaded.

"My God, Lyle!" Barr's voice had lost its resonance and found a new and higher range. He folded his hands and held them up toward Lyle in the manner of an Oriental greeting. "You're a fair man, you can't do this."

Hedman jammed the end of the barrel into Barr's chest and backed him up. Barr nodded quickly, as if agreeing to an urgently given order. His lips moved silently.

Gun said, "Lyle!" and took a step forward.

"Reuben!" Hedman ordered. The dog rose from the grass at Hedman's feet, compressed its body back into its hindquarters. It uncoiled into the air and shot straight toward Gun's face. Gun leaned forward, locked his elbows. With both hands he caught hold of Reuben's hard neck. The animal's driving weight jolted him, but he held fast. Reuben's claws slashed at Gun's face and arms and chest. His teeth snapped like breaking ice. Gun found the dog's windpipe with his left hand and squeezed it with all the power he could force into his damaged fist. Holding the animal in the air with one arm, he speared his right hand through the dog's flailing legs and took firm hold on a rear thigh. He lifted Reuben high above his head. The dog twisted crazily and clawed at the sky. Its tail went round and round like the blade of a fan. Gun sucked his lungs full of air, exhaled a roar, and brought the dog down spine first onto a bent knee. It sounded like the cracking of a great branch, and then Reuben was on the ground, spastic, jerking, twitching one foot, whining. His long body was bent the wrong way into a perfect vee, front and back legs pointing in opposite directions.

Hedman and Barr looked from Reuben to Gun, then at one another. Hedman raised the shotgun and put the barrel six inches from the minister's chest. An orange fire burst from the gun's mouth and the report was sharp yet muffled, like a firecracker under a heavy blanket. Reverend Barr hopped backward, raised a single finger, then fell to his side, and his head cracked against the stone boathouse.

39

Carol bolted toward the fallen minister, but Fraser blocked her way, deer rifle in his hands. Carol crossed her pale wrists in front of her breasts. Her slender fingers were spread wide. She slowly turned and stared at Hedman. In the light from the Coleman lamp, Gun could see Carol's eyes blinking, a muscle ticking rhythmically in her jaw. She was working for control. That's right, Carol, Gun thought, keep a tight rein. He looked at Mazy, two steps to his left. She was staring at Hedman too, but not blinking, not fighting panic. She didn't even look surprised. Gun stepped toward her and took hold of her cool hand.

"You're over the edge, Lyle," Gun said quietly.

Lyle didn't answer. He was looking down at his dog, thoroughly dead now. A fish jumped in the water not far away. Hedman's men watched their boss. Geoff stood stiff as a soldier.

Jack, on Gun's right, stood closest to the boathouse. Now he put an arm out and struck a leaning pose against the corner. The dead minister lay several feet in front of him. "Tell you what, Lyle." Jack's voice was so deep and loud in the silence that Hedman jerked. "You're going to find out what people think of you around here. There'll be an investigation from the outside, because people on the inside are going to demand it." Jack aimed one of his short fingers like a pistol. "Wait. See."

Hedman's face knotted up, went slack. He sighed like a man fresh from running eight flights of stairs. Gun looked at Jack, and their eyes met in a glimmer of understanding and determination. Hedman was coming unlatched. There would be a way to take advantage of him, a way out of this—if everyone could just stay calm and move fast when the moment arrived. It was a matter of applying pressure at the weak point.

Gun pulled Mazy close. "Geoff," he said, "you really came through for Daddy this time. I've gotta admit that was a nice little stunt you pulled in the restaurant. You've got two prongs in the wall after all. So why don't you do your old man a favor and tell him he's way over his head? Or do yourself a favor. Make the right decision now and you buy yourself a future. I think you're smart enough to know that."

Geoff lifted his chin and frowned. He turned to his father. Lyle shivered once and looked around bright-eyed, like a man coming to. His eyes settled on Gun and he seemed to find his focus. "Better talk while you can, Pedersen, because we're going to put you and Jack to sleep here in just a few minutes. Boys"— Hedman swung Jack's shotgun around like a pointing stick—"let's get things going. We need two boats. Berg, Fraser, get Pedersen's boat out of that shed and into the lake. Horseley, help me keep an eye on these folks here. Move them out of the way, give the boys a chance to work." Lyle's voice was louder than it needed to be.

Hedman and Horseley moved everyone to the edge of the lake next to the dock, sat them down on the rocks. Gun squeezed Mazy's shoulder. She fastened her grip around his fingers.

Berg and Fraser rolled the boat down to the lake on its trailer and fiddled with the crank release. Hedman was silent. Several times he peered back through the darkness toward the bodies of Reverend Barr and Reuben.

"Shit," said Fraser, bending over the crank mechanism at the front of the trailer.

"Hurry up with that!" Hedman yelled.

"It's stuck or something," Berg said.

"Then break it, you asshole!" Lyle stormed over to the boat. "Here, lean on this, Berg. Put that fat to use. And move it!"

Whatever was stuck gave to Berg's weight. Lyle strutted back to where Horseley stood playing guard. He was monkeying nervously with his long-barreled .45, cocking and uncocking it, cocking it again. He jerked it momentarily toward Geoff. "Mr. Hedman, say, how come your kid don't have a gun? What's he supposed to be doing? Just standing there?" Geoff stood with his hands in his pockets next to the Coleman lamp. He looked like a man who'd just seen an unhappy vision of the future. The proud line of his shoulders had fallen. They hung from his neck like a broken clothes hanger.

Hedman moistened his lips, then spoke carefully, enunciating each word. His eyes blazed. "You keep that ugly face of yours shut, Horseley, and quit playing around with that cowboy gun. Shoot somebody with it, and I have Berg break your back. Do you understand?"

Horseley looked away.

"I said, do you understand."

Horseley adjusted the tilt of his shoulders. "Yeah," he said.

"Good."

"Lyle," Jack said, lifting himself to a squat. "Tell me. If you're so worried about using guns, what's to stop us from just hopping into one of these boats here and cruising into town?"

"On your ass, LaSalle." Hedman wiggled the barrel of the shotgun.

Jack lowered himself to the rocks. "Question stands," he said.

"Plan B. Worse for me, worse for you. Well, maybe not worse for you. If it comes to shooting you or letting you go, I don't have a lot of choice at this point, do I?"

Berg and Fraser had Gun's boat in the water and were trying to get the motor started. Berg was standing in the back of the boat and yanking the starter rope.

"Now this damn engine won't start!" Fraser said. Just then it fired, started sputtering, shaking, and smoking. But running.

"Good work, boys." Gun raised his voice above the engine's. "I haven't been able to start it for weeks."

Hedman studied Gun out the corner of his eye for a few seconds, then called out, "Keep that motor running, Fraser. Hand on the throttle. Berg, you bring that medicine bag and your big butt over here. Right now."

Berg stepped from the boat to the dock and walked to Hedman's side. He handed over a small black bag resembling a shaving kit. Lyle signaled for Geoff, handed him the shotgun. Geoff moved toward the lake and propped himself into a guardlike stance in front of Gun. Lyle opened the black bag and removed a syringe. He held it up before his face, the needle brilliant in the lamplight.

"Ever gone under the knife, Gun? How about you, Jack?" Hedman was yelling over the racket of the boat motor. "I have. Twice. For an appendectomy when I was fifteen and a hernia at forty-five. Both times I thoroughly enjoyed the preoperation bliss induced by this little baby." He waved the needle. "This stuff comes straight from heaven. It's beautiful. Really, I'm envious. The girls should be too. See, it so happens Berg here only brought enough for two injections, instead of four like I told him. And I'd say floating away on the magic serum is a small bit sweeter than getting brained by a chunk of stone. What do you think, Carol?" Hedman closed his eyes, shook his head in mock sorrow. "I've got to use it on the boys, of course. Hope you understand. Somehow I just don't think I can trust them not to try something brave once we get out on the water."

Jack said, "We'd be good as gold, Lyle."

Gun squeezed Mazy's shoulder. He could feel her tension but knew she'd hold up. Weakness never showed in her, and for the first time he was thankful for that. On the other side of Mazy, Jack leaned forward and nodded. His face wore the schoolyard smile again, a half grin of anticipation. His eyes were ready, hard and sparkling.

Carol was looking at the ground, mouth drawn flat. Under his breath Gun told her, "Things are going to happen fast. Get a good grip," and Carol smiled, brave and accusatory.

"Okay," Lyle said, "I want you and you"—he pointed with his nose at Berg and Horseley—"to grab hold of the big man there and keep him steady. These pinpricks hurt sometimes." Hedman flourished the needle in the light of the Coleman lamp. "Bring him over here," he said.

Gun kissed Mazy on the cheek and stood up. As he reached down to touch Carol on the shoulder he remembered the fish-cleaning knife. What the hell had she done with it? He pressed her shoulder and she looked up, then Berg and Horseley were at his sides. They pushed him forward into the bright circle of lamplight. Lyle's face looked thinner and sharper, lit from below. "Shirt off," he said.

Gun took off the wool Pendleton and felt the chill air brighten his skin. Couldn't be more than forty degrees, he thought. Horseley tucked the .45 in his pants and locked both hands around Gun's right arm. Gun could feel the pitch of the man's nerves, tight as stretched wire. Berg was another matter, all that weight. The giant had his shotgun in his left hand, Gun's arm in his right. He was like something immovable, a jutting piece of bedrock, and he smelled like a hamburger starting to go bad.

As Hedman knelt beside the lamp and fumbled with the black bag, Gun measured distances. Straight ahead thirty feet Fraser and his sunglasses sat in the Alumacraft, playing the throttle, deer rifle handy. Geoff stood a few yards off to the left; Jack, Carol, and Mazy were on the right. Geoff had the gun butted against his hip and pointed at Jack, but Gun doubted he'd use it. No barrels on Gun. Almost time.

Hedman said, "Okay," then stood up, the needle ready. "Relax those biceps, now, be brave," he crooned.

Horseley and Berg tightened down. "Jack," Gun said, "you're right behind me."

Jack nodded and blinked. Gun saw his friend's hand close around a baseball-sized rock next to his knee. Hedman stepped to Gun's side. "Keep him there, boys," he said.

Gun tensed. The icy sphere expanding beneath his heart was so light and buoyant he felt it might lift him off the ground. He watched for the glint of the needle. Saw it.

Now.

40

He released himself into motion, clamped the fingers of his right hand on Horseley's belt, used his own weight as a fulcrum. Horseley came up like a feed sack over Gun's shoulder and into Hedman's face. The needle flew. Berg lifted his shotgun but Gun brought up his knee, and the giant bent double over a ruined groin. Gun sprinted for the boat. He was three strides back of Jack, one behind Mazy and Carol. Geoff was on his back on the ground, a red lump growing under one eye.

Fraser was still in the boat. Gun saw Jack get there first, rifle fire lighting the air, and launch a flying cross-body. Then Fraser's feet were pointing straight up and his body was hitting the water and Jack was yelling "stay low" and throwing the women into the bottom of the boat. Gun freed the tie line and jumped. Jack throttled wide open and swung the bow into the fog. Gun couldn't see more than fifty feet.

"Damn this motor!" Jack yelled. He had it full

throttle and was messing with the lean-rich dial, trying to coax out more power. Mazy and Carol lay in the center of the boat. Gun sat on the rear seat next to Jack, their weight pulling the bow off the water for speed.

Behind them the headlight beam of Young's runabout swung like a long pole across the water, then flared into a spot.

"The islands," Gun said.

Jack nodded. The town of Stony was five miles to the south, too far. But the cluster of four islands lay only a mile due west and offered hundreds of places to hide: small bays lined with overhanging limbs, old abandoned cabins, hollow caves in the washed-out shorelines. If they could beat Hedman to the islands, they might elude him till morning.

A rifle shot rang across the water and whined overhead. Gun and Jack slid off the seat to the floor. Jack kept his hand on the stick and his head just high enough to hold a straight line. The runabout was coming on in a hurry. Gun could already make out the silhouettes of the men on board. Five. A second shot ripped into the stern, not a foot from Gun's face.

The islands were a couple hundred yards off when the big boat came roaring up alongside. Berg raised himself over the windshield of the runabout, shotgun in hand. Jack threw the Alumacraft into a steep bank, straightened out again. The runabout stayed right on them. Again Berg positioned for a shot, and again Jack banked, this time in the other direction. Berg fired. The shot was like thunder, and pellets sprayed the boat's high-riding side. Jack kept the port gunwale running flush on the water, the starboard high in the air, and scribed a tight circle in the water. Horseley followed with the runabout, drawing a close line around them. They were near enough for Gun to see Geoff's bloodied face at Berg's shoulder.

After two complete circles Jack rammed the stick all the way over. The bow hopped out of the water, lurched around like the arm of a crane, and broke off in a wild tangent directly toward the broadside of the runabout.

On impact the bow of the Alumacraft split wide open. The little boat stood up on the water proud as a pine tree. Gun landed free of the wreckage, headfirst. When he surfaced his boat was lying behind him, upside down on the water. Ahead, the runabout's light bent toward him in a fast arc, coming hard. He couldn't tell if anyone was still in it. Then in the boat's lighted path he saw the head of a swimmer, heard a loud thump as the head went down before the charging prow. He dove deep, his own heart crashing in his ears.

The boat passed overhead and Gun surfaced. He swam hard toward the bobbing lump in the water. He didn't allow himself to think. Somewhere behind him there was splashing, a man's scream, a low grunt that sounded like Jack. Gun reached the floating body in a dozen fast strokes. The head was facedown, long hair fanning out on the water. The skull had been cleft open like a notched melon. No blood, only sharp white bone and spongy-looking brain. Gun lifted the face and looked into the staring eyes of Fraser. His sunglasses covered his mouth.

"Thank God," Gun whispered. "Mazy! Jack! Carol!" he yelled. No answer. Just more splashing, labored breathing, a curse. It seemed to come from behind the turtled Alumacraft. Gun swam toward it, then stopped dead in the water as the sound of the runabout started growing louder again. He looked up. The boat was returning, slowly now, and a tall figure stood behind the wheel. Lyle Hedman. As the boat came on, Gun could see where Jack had rammed it.

The gash was in the middle of the port side, well above the waterline.

Gun kept his arms and legs moving steadily and held his head low. He prepared to dive again. Then a face appeared above the water, just a dozen feet away, in front of the tipped Alumacraft. Jack? Gun couldn't tell. The boat's light came closer and sharpened his vision. It was Horseley in the water, and his eyes were fastened on Gun. The headlight moved in. Gun saw Horseley's .45 on the surface of the lake, saw the small round hole of the barrel. Then a shadow appeared from behind Horseley and a line of bright silver flashed beneath Horseley's chin. A stream of blood arced from his neck. The shadow withdrew beneath the boat. Horseley slipped out of sight. Gun locked air in his chest and dove away from the runabout, remembering the fish-cleaning knife. Carol.

Hedman's shotgun boomed. Pellets hit the water and rattled off the aluminum hull of the capsized boat. Gun dove deep and pushed hard for the sound of Hedman's slowing motor. He kicked his feet violently, thrust his arms forward and back, forward and back. His lungs burned. The runabout was barely moving now, the engine idling. Gun swam beneath it and came up on the other side, sucked his lungs full without making a sound. He fastened his fingers on the gunwale and pulled down with everything he had. The boat rocked hard and Hedman fell toward the rear, managing to hang onto his shotgun but landing facefirst in the twisted snarls of anchor rope.

Gun vaulted over the side and landed off balance on hip and elbow beneath the steering wheel and throttle lever. Hedman tossed off coils of rope and pushed himself to his knees. Both men reached their feet at the same moment. Hedman—just eight feet away, a circle of rope hanging from his neck—held the shotgun at his waist, barrel toward Gun's chest.

Gun said, "It was a nice idea, Lyle." He felt behind him for the throttle, found it.

"This part is still nice," Lyle said. He smiled.

Gun jammed the lever to full power and threw himself free of the boat. Hedman flipped backward into the water and blasted a red hole in the sky. Gun swam toward him as the boat charged away. He reached him, put a hand on his shoulder, then Lyle's neck popped like a cork and the rope yanked him into the air. The motor roared a moment's resistance, then Lyle was gone, horizontal on the water, flying, arms and legs bouncing on the surface of the lake like empty cans thrown from a speeding car. He was heading straight for town.

Gun swam toward the wreckage of his old boat. He couldn't hear the splashing anymore. "Mazy!" he called.

"Dad!"

He tried to pinpoint her voice. It came again. "Dad!" Then he could see her, swimming toward him in the foggy darkness. She had two heads.

"Mazy . . ."

Now Gun could see she was swimming arm-in-arm with Jack, helping and being helped, the two of them negotiating a sort of double sidestroke. Jack's face ran with blood. Gun met them beside the capsized boat, at the place where Horseley had gone under.

"You're all right?" Gun said.

Jack was breathing hard, but he forced a smile and showed Gun a new black space in his top row of teeth. "Wouldn't be, if your girl hadn't clubbed that caveman with an oar. He was too much for me. Hell, it was like trying to drown an island."

"He got away, took off swimming that way," said Mazy, pointing. Then her eyes went black with fear. "Where's Carol?"

"Carol's fine, I believe. Isn't that right, Carol?" Gun said, lifting his voice.

A soft splash sounded from underneath the boat, and Carol surfaced between Mazy and Gun. Wet hair covered her face like a striped mask. Gun pushed the hair from her eyes, then lifted her right arm into the air. In her fist she held the fish-cleaning knife with the slender, curving blade.

41

It was two days later, Thursday morning, seven o'clock. The sun was clean white and shining through the trees. A storm had passed through in the night, leaving the air calm and purified. Gun finished his morning swim and walked ashore. He was wearing only a pair of gray longjohns. Stony Lake was still very cold.

He took a towel from where it hung on a dock post and dried his chest and shoulders. He was rubbing his hair dry when he heard Carol's voice.

"Still in your longies, I see."

Gun looked up and saw her in the outfield grass. Even from twenty yards he could tell her green eyes were rested. Her black hair shone. Beside her was her son Michael, whom Gun had met the day before. He had his mother's long legs and someone else's face, a rugged face, wide cheekbones, a bony nose. Gun joined them on the grass and shook hands with Michael.

"We've got some news," Carol said. "They found Berg, and Geoff too." Berg and Geoff had been the only two unaccounted for since the other night. The search had been large and well-publicized.

"Together, were they?" asked Gun.

"Far from it. Berg was hiding in Nick Faris's barn, up in the haymow. State police bloodhounds found him last night, about eleven-thirty." Carol touched Gun's arm. "We'd better get you inside, you've got goose bumps."

"What about Geoff?"

Michael put an arm around his mother's shoulders. Carol said, "Geoff washed up on the town beach. Early this morning."

Gun turned toward the lake. "That was a strong wind we had. Came straight out of the north." He pictured Geoff's face, bloated and tanless, forced it out of his mind.

After a moment Carol said, "Michael and I were wondering if you and Mazy would like to go out, get some breakfast."

"Can't you smell anything?" said Gun, turning toward them again. Carol and Michael put their noses in the air. "That's Mazy's bacon frying."

Four plates of bacon, eggs, and hash browns later, they sat at Gun's pine table sipping strong stove-top coffee. Yesterday they'd all been obliged to tell their stories over and over again—to investigators from the FBI and the state crime bureau, to media folks of every stripe. Mazy had phoned an exclusive to the *Tribune,* which had appeared this morning under a headline an inch tall. Today was a breather. There had been several minutes of silence when someone belted Gun's door, boom boom boom, and an enormous voice bawled, "Gun Pedersen, you home?"

Mike blinked at his mother, who lifted her shoulders. Mazy said, "Beats me." Gun smiled, took a long plug of coffee and stood from the table.

Bowser was clean-shaven and round-headed, grinning. The bottom several buttons of his red flannel shirt were missing and his big hairy belly looked like somebody's naked rear end backing out of a tent. "Went into that cutesy barber shop of Loretta's last night," he said. They were standing next to home plate. Behind them a celebration of summer birds swirled in the white pine. "Went in and sat down and told them, I don't want bald but I want its first cousin."

"You're improved," Gun said.

"Talk in town is all Gun Pedersen," Bowser said.

"Great."

"You done a job on 'em," said Bowser. His left eye held respectfully on Gun's face while the right went wandering off toward the lake. "Done a job on Hedman, may he fry on the Big Griddle. Done a job on the old Loon Mall. I'm admiring of that, Gun."

"Come in for breakfast?"

"Naw. You got folks over." Bowser stood in the bird-wild noise of the morning, hands in his pockets, breathing easily. A swell of far-off laughter came from the house, Mazy and Carol and Mike.

"I felt real bad about missing your dad's funeral," Gun said. "I thought about it a lot that day."

Bowser shifted his weight from one thick leg to the other, shot a stream of saliva at home plate. "Hard to be in two places at once. And you didn't miss a hell of a lot. Arnie Quinn at the funeral parlor don't waste no time. A couple of tunes and a prayer, and Arnie and his helper roll 'em right out to the limo. Best thing about it all was the taps at the graveyard. That trumpet player, now, he knew how to make a pretty sound. I loved that."

They were quiet. Bowser took one hand from his pocket and peeked at the dirt under his nails, then looked evenly at Gun. His eyes almost seemed to focus on the same point, nearly came together to function as a matched pair. "You're welcome at the home place, Gun. Anytime."

"Thanks."

The kitchen was relaxed and gold with sun when Gun stepped back inside. Mike was leaning into the refrigerator, reading a buttermilk carton. Mazy rested back in her chair, eyes closed. Carol folded the newspaper she held and looked a question at Gun. He raised his arms and held them out from his sides, palms up.

"Happy day," he said.

FROM THE BESTSELLING AUTHOR OF
ALICE IN LA LA LAND

ROBERT
CAMPBELL

From Edgar Award-Winning author Robert
Campbell come big time crime novels with
a brilliant kaleidoscope of characters.

☐ *ALICE IN LA LA LAND* ....66931/$3.95

☐ *RED CENT* ....64364/$3.50

☐ *PLUGGED NICKEL* ....64363/$3.50

☐ *JUICE* ....67454/$4.95

SWEET LA-LA LAND *Now Available*
In Hardcover From **Poseiden Press**

POCKET
B O O K S